Eighty-Eight Keys

Catherine Lavender

Whimsical Publications, LLC

Florida

Eighty-Eight Keys is a work of fiction. Names, characters, and incidents are the products of the author's imagination and are either fictitious or are used fictitiously. Any resemblance to actual events or persons, living or dead, is entirely coincidental.

To purchase the authorized electronic edition of *Eighty-Eight Keys*, visit www.whimsicalpublications.com

Cover art by Traci Markou
Editing by Brieanna Robertson
Line editing by Janet Durbin

Published in the United States by
Whimsical Publications, LLC
Florida

ISBN-13: 978-1-936167-83-8

Printed in the United States of America

The jarring ring of the telephone pulled Leah back into the present. It took her a couple of rings to find the buried cell phone. "Hello?"

"Hey, Leah, it's Quincy. I was just calling to check up on you."

She settled back into a small section of the couch. "Hi, Quincy. I'm doing okay."

"You sure?" She could hear the concern in his voice. "You sound a little sad."

The picture of her and Jason crumpled in her fist. "Well, you know how it is. I'm surrounded by ghosts at every turn." Her inner voice urged her to change the subject quickly. "How are you doing?"

"Well, that kind of brings me to the second purpose of this call. Would you mind coming in this afternoon? There is still so much to do for the gala, and we can use all the help we can get."

Leah looked at her watch, then at the mess in her living room. "Yep, I can be there in a couple of hours."

Saying her goodbyes, Leah hung up the phone and made a mental note to pick up, packing boxes along the way. When her lease was up, she was moving to her neon oasis—Las Vegas. Leah was going to be a pianist.

Running thirty minutes late, Leah pulled into the parking lot of Bright Horizons Youth Group. She didn't see Mrs. Turner and Rosa until she almost collided into them.

"Oh, oops, sorry," Leah said, fumbling with her purse and notebook. "I, um, didn't see you there." The look on Rosa's face was pure anger.

"Well, we are certainly glad you're here," Mrs. Turner said with an airy smile. "There is just so much that needs to be done, and well, it is your business to know how to do this."

Leah smiled, situating her purse on her shoulder, and avoided eye contact with Rosa in case one of the thousand daggers thrown from her eyes would penetrate. "You know, I am just happy to help," she said to the older woman. Leah cringed at the overly eager sound of her own voice.

"And we are so glad you are helping, swallowing your pride for the good of Bright Horizons." Mrs. Turner wore her Armani dress like it was a second skin, her makeup and hair flawless as always. Her smile was etched, and didn't quite spread to the rest of her face.

"I don't understand why..." Rosa said. Her hostility spoke volumes.

Leah braced herself for a very vocal confrontation.

"No, dear." Mrs. Turner put a beautifully manicured hand on Rosa's forearm. "You don't understand, and you never will if you don't check your attitude."

A car horn caused all three women to look around. "Ah, that's for me." Mrs. Turner pulled a sheet of paper from her book, not acknowledging the impatient student honking.

Leah didn't want to know why the University's current basketball star was sitting in Mrs. Turner's car.

"If you both will excuse me, I have more important matters to attend to." She handed Leah a long list, "Be a dear and see if you can crank this out."

The two women eyed each other warily.

Rosa brushed past Leah. "Don't you dare screw this up," she hissed.

"Why would you think that?" Leah usually kept to herself as far as Rosa was concerned, but the implication bothered her.

Rosa slid on a pair of sunglasses. "Because you screw everything up."

Dedicated to:

Susie Mae McCray
&
Ola Mae Lavender

You have always encouraged my heart with unconditional love.

Acknowledgement

I would like to give a heartfelt thanks to my family for their continuous encouragement and support.

I wish to express my sincere thanks to both Renee M. Moon and Hillary Davis. They have both been a strong support system throughout this whole process, and believed in my vision for Eighty-Eight keys.

I would also like to extend my sense of gratitude to one and all who directly or indirectly gave me the courage and inspiration to write my debut novel Eighty-Eight Keys.

Being an author has been a childhood dream, and I'm grateful for the opportunity to live and share my passion.

Prologue

Theresa Jordan walked quickly along her route, chastising herself for running behind. She silently cursed the Wilsons' dog for scaring her out of five precious minutes. "Maintain the schedule," she muttered, marching up the walkway. "*Respect the schedule!*"

Her hand was poised to rap hard, but the door slowly swung open on the first knock. "Hello?" She yelled loudly, "I have a delivery here."

When there was no answer, she reached for the *Sorry I Missed You* pad when the sound of rushing water stopped her. "Hello?"

She called again, her senses on high alert. "Is anybody home?" Stepping cautiously into the front room, Theresa looked around. "Hello?" She called out again, "Mail carrier, I have a delivery."

The living room seemed to be in order, decently decorated, she supposed, but there was something in the air. A scent that made her hackles rise.

Slowly, she followed the sound of running water in the large, gourmet kitchen. Theresa came around the counter and found the tap in the sink flowing into a glass vase of white lilies. She reached over to turn the tap off, opened her mouth to yell again, and then saw drops of red dripping off the stainless steel sink. Her heart began to beat faster. A splash of green caught her eye, and as she looked over, she spotted a bloody knife lying next to a wicker bowl that was neatly piled with green apples.

The voice in her head told her to run away fast, but she never did what the voice in her head told her.

Moving slowly toward the back of the house, the air shifted and changed. It felt surprisingly empty, as empty as a heart that refused to love. The air was thick, stuffy, and suffocating any real emotion. *But there was something else.*

Once in the bedroom, she knew what the smell was, what the feeling was. Death. There was also an unmistakable hint of Channel No. 5. The scent tiptoed around the room, a seemingly innocent bystander, but strong enough to own the space.

Sheets on the bed, once a dazzling white, pure as newly fallen snow, were splattered in crimson, a horrific sinful crimson that had set in and made itself at home. Theresa stood frozen out of fear, waiting for the mangled body to speak to her. To tell her who did this unspeakable act. Instead the silence was broken by the ringing of a cell phone that was out of reach on a nightstand.

The ghastly look in the corpse eyes broke Theresa's trance. She ran as fast as she could away from the sight and the smell of murder.

Chapter One

Leah opened her sore eyes and quickly closed them again. She feared the throbbing in her head would escalate with the sunlight pouring through her bedroom window. Getting out of bed was a struggle; her body felt the physical and emotional turmoil with each small movement she made. The thin blanket on her bed felt like a slab of concrete covering her, heavy and immovable.

After struggling for several minutes, her feet made it to the cool wood floor. It took several more minutes of internal debate before she cleared the safety of her bed and went to face the cruel world that awaited her.

Quickly entering the bathroom, Leah avoided looking at the mirror. She could feel her eyes were swollen from crying, she didn't need it confirmed. Her hand reached for the shower tap and turned it to scalding. Shedding the clothes she had worn since yesterday, Leah stepped into the steamy water, praying that the shower would wash away the anguish that she felt.

Leah dressed slowly; the shower only washed away the physical grime. The emotional filth still clung to her, and every movement she made took effort. Finally facing the mirror, she applied makeup to the dark circles under her eyes and the blotchiness around her face. The hairbrush ran through her dark layers of hair with ease and she dabbed a bit of perfume behind her neck and ears.

Giving her reflection a critical eye, Leah knew all eyes were going to be on her today and she had to look as though she had it together. The classic little black J. Crew dress made her look smart and sophisticated. Looping a strand of pearls around her long, slender neck, Leah nodded and whispered, "You can do this." With another nod at her reflection, she said it again. "You *can* do this."

Memories rushed through her head so fast she gripped the vanity before her knees gave way under the weight of emotion. Lowering her body into a nearby chair, Leah indulged in the sweet memory of the first time she met Jason Rowe, and how he stole her heart with one captivating smile...

Leaving home had not been easy for Leah, but she finally made the break to go away to graduate school. Her new-found freedom from her strict religious upbringing was exhilarating and overwhelming. Makeup, which was regarded as a sinful indulgence of loose women while she was growing up, was now a necessity before leaving for classes.

"Clothing was meant to cover the flesh," so her mother intoned repeatedly, but Leah enjoyed wearing fun, flirty clothes that hugged her curves a little. It attracted male attention, which she found a secret thrill as her confidence grew, but she still felt shy and awkward around men. Leah wondered if she would ever grow beyond the nerdy, avid churchgoer her parents had raised.

One of Leah's classmates had informed her that no self-respecting woman would deprive her closet of the LBD—it was a necessity. Curiosity won out over self-consciousness as Leah asked the inevitable, what exactly was an LBD? She had never seen anyone's eyes grow as large as her classmate's when she asked. The sputtering response was, "a little black dress, of course!" Apparently, every woman needed a little black dress in their closet; it goes with everything. The next morning, Leah was out searching for her very first LBD.

While out searching, Leah never realized that two very tall men watched her every move from across the street.

Stopping at the corner coffee house, Leah assessed the line of people and crossed her fingers there would be a cheese Danish left as she waited impatiently for her turn to order. There were three left in the case, and eight people in front of her. With her eyes glued on the yummy pastry, she mentally calculated the calories and reminded herself the gym was not on her schedule for the day. Although she was not a total health nut, health was important to her. Leah's mouth salivated as she stepped forward. There were still three Danishes left and six people in line as she guesstimated the caloric shift in her daily eating habit to accommodate the treat.

A voice behind her startled her back into reality. "Was your father a thief?"

Leah turned her head toward the voice. Her eyes trailed upwards to a very tall, good-looking man, "I'm sorry?" She could feel the heat rise in her face. "Did you say something?"

He nodded. "I did. I asked if your father was a thief."

Leah shook her head slowly. "No, my father is a Pentecostal minister." She turned back to the display case and breathed a sigh of relief when she saw there were still three Danishes in the case and five people ahead of her.

"Oh," the man behind her said. "So, you are a preacher's kid?"

She turned quickly again to answer. "Yes, you could say that I am." Leah looked up into his face and she felt her heart thud up into her throat as he smiled. With that one act, his eyes lit up and his face brightened. Suddenly, the Danish didn't seem as important.

"I'm Jason, by the way." He rolled the basketball he carried into his left hand to shake with his right. "Jason Rowe."

"Leah," she said, mesmerized by his handsome smile.

The line moved again. "Can I buy you a cup of coffee?"

"Sure!" She was a little surprised at how quickly she agreed.

"Great, grab us a table and I'll meet you. What did you want?"

"I was going to get a tall latte with one half shot of regular espresso and one half shot of decaf, a half a shot of sugar-free hazelnut syrup, skim milk with extra foam."

"Skim milk? Not half and half?" His teasing made her feel self-conscious and he quickly amended his quip. "I'm sorry. I didn't mean to hurt your feelings."

"You didn't," she lied, forcing a smile. It felt false, but she hoped it looked genuine. "I get weird looks all the time when I order coffee." Another lie and she could feel the flames of hell licking at her feet. "I see a table over there." She pointed as another tall man joined Jason.

"Hey," Jason said to the man. "This is Leah." He introduced her as if she was the only person in the coffee shop. "Leah, this is Quincy, a frequent interloper and usurper of potential dates."

"Man, that just isn't cool," Quincy griped as he offered his hand to Leah. "It is nice to meet you."

Leah thought he was boyishly handsome, but his smile didn't quite reach his eyes. "Jason, I'll meet you on the court in an hour." Quincy grabbed Jason's hand and pulled him forward in some sort of shoulder-bump, guy thing Leah didn't quite understand. Quincy whispered something into his friend's ear. Jason laughed and Leah felt mildly irritated.

"It was nice to meet you," Quincy said before leaving the coffee shop.

"And I think you better go claim our table." Jason pointed at a couple who looked very lost, seemingly searching for a place to sit.

Leah moved quickly to the seat before the couple could claim it and snapped open the abandoned newspaper left by the previous occupant. With her head bent over an article on the new pianist in the University's symphony orchestra, Leah slyly watched the couple who gave her an evil eye as they passed. Shifting her glance to Jason, Leah watched him tossing the basketball from one hand to the next, waiting for his turn. Turning his head slowly, they made eye contact and he gave her a bright smile that made her stomach flip. She pulled her gaze back to the newspaper, reached around, and dug in her large purse. Fingers closing around the cool metal object, she secretly brought it out and flipped it open.

"Hair, decent," she muttered, shifting her face around to look into the small mirror. "Nose, not shiny," she said softly. Leah saw Jason heading in her direction, quickly closed the mirror, and slid it back into her purse.

"One Leah special," he said, setting the coffee cup down with a flourish. He then presented her with the coveted pastry she had been eyeing. "You look like a cheese Danish kind of girl," he said with a sheepish grin.

Leah was amazed he knew exactly what she wanted. "Thank you." She slid the plate closer to her.

He shrugged, setting his own coffee down in front of him. "It was nothing. I had to fight a member of the debate team for it."

"Well I appreciate the effort." She pulled apart the Danish, popped a piece in her mouth, and savored the sweetness. "Would you like some?"

He held up an apologetic hand. "No, thank you." He patted

his stomach. "It would go straight to my belly." The wattage of his smile seemed to brighten.

Leah took a sip of coffee. "Oh, perfect, most people get it wrong. What did you get?"

"Same as you." He shifted the cup to the side.

"I hope you like it." She took another sip before asking, "Why did you ask if my father was a thief?"

Red splotches appeared on his cheeks. "Oh, that." He shifted uncomfortably in his chair and chuckled nervously. "Well, that was kind of Quincy's fault."

"How so?"

"We had just read an article on cheesy pick-up lines, and thought we'd...well, he thought we should experiment."

"So I was your guinea pig?" She wasn't sure if she was flattered or mortified.

"Not really," he answered quickly. "I wanted to talk to you either way. I saw you go into Schwartz Music before you came in here."

"So now you're a stalker?" Turning the tables on his teasing was kind of fun, she decided.

"Sort of," he laughed. "Except..." His face grew redder. "You know what?" His smile was even more endearing when he was embarrassed. "I think we need to start this meeting again."

Leah surprised herself, again, by grabbing his arm to keep him seated. "No, I want to hear the cheesy pick-up line."

He sighed in mock irritation. "All right, fine, but you asked for it." Shifting in his chair, he straightened and said in a cheesy sort of voice, "Is your father a thief? Because he stole the stars and put them in your eyes."

"Seriously? That is what you were going to use?" She wasn't sure where the ease of her demeanor was coming from, but she wanted to find it and wedge the door open permanently.

He shrugged. "The article didn't say it was effective."

She took another sip. "You haven't touched your coffee; is it okay?"

"I'm not really a coffee drinker, but for some reason I wanted to come to this place." He pushed the beverage towards Leah. "I'd do just about anything for an excuse to talk to a beautiful woman..."

Even as she made the shift back into reality, Leah could smell a faint whiff of the Burberry Cologne Jason wore. Slowly unfolding her hands from the death grip she had on the vanity, Leah flexed her fingers to circulate them.

"Jason would say you were being silly," she muttered to the reflection in the mirror. "I need to get past this." The problem was she didn't know how she was going to accomplish that.

"Jason, Jason, Jason." She shook her head, mumbling his name, remembering that she had loved him so deeply. From the beginning of their friendship to the end, when he shattered her heart into a thousand slivers, she loved him. Leah found him to be an extremely generous friend, but a very selfish lover. "Was it really love or severe, blinding infatuation?" she asked herself as she stared at her gaunt face in the mirror. Leah supposed she was in love because she was always finding the strength to pick up the pieces of her heart. That was until that final day when the debris of heartbreak was too vast and scattered to collect.

Arriving late to the church, Leah hurried up the stone steps and stopped short in the entryway. Jason's life unfolded before her in a series of framed photographs. A montage of happy grins gave her goose bumps as she made the walk down memory lane. A photo of Jason at the age of three, holding up a basketball that was bigger than him, made her smile. His father knelt next to him, looking as proud as any father would.

Kind words were offered to her by the Mayor, community leaders, and his peers. They praised Jason for his civic accomplishments, his college achievements, and post-college life. Admiration for Jason poured from the front of the sanctuary as colleagues praised him for his generous spirit while developing and running a youth basketball organization called Bright Horizons Youth Group, an organization intended to help adolescents academically and to encourage scouting talent. Leah couldn't help but smile when she heard that. Jason was so proud when finding a "diamond in the rough."

The tightness in her chest intensified as she moved closer

to the sanctuary. She could see from the large wooden doorway the massive floral displays, tall, cream-colored pillar candles, and photographs displayed everywhere. Leah chanced running her finger lovingly over the picture of Jason with his mother and three sisters at a family reunion. There were also college basketball photos with teammates and several with Coach Turner. The more recent photos showed Jason at a dinner party, dressed in a tuxedo laughing with a woman who eyes sparkled with infatuation, a feeling Leah could easily relate to. Rosa, the woman in the picture, had become an obstacle that tarnished the relationship Leah once had with Jason. Another photo included one with a toddler perched on Jason's shoulder. Leah's heart constricted as she realized little Jay-Jay would be three years old next month—and his father would not be there to celebrate.

With the eulogies concluded, Leah could see a few people rise and proceed to the front of the altar to pay their final respects. She took a deep breath, steeled her spine, and made her way forward. The *click, click, click* of her heels on the scuffed wood floor echoed throughout the sanctuary, where lost souls were tormented, and redeemed souls rested in peace. Eyes turned in her direction and bodies scurried out of her way as she walked the same path of both sanctified believers and condemned sinners.

A large, wooden cross was nailed to the wall above the altar. It served as her beacon, a focal point to avoid the reality of Jason's death. Christ, cloaked in crimson, a crown of thorns piercing into his brow—his suffering was what she concentrated on, not the open hostility that was waiting for her from Rosa. The animosity toward her was oppressive, but Leah kept her eyes fixed on the Lord. She knew there was judgment toward her, but willed her feet to move forward, allowing her heart to overrule the judgment.

Small movements to her right caused Leah to lose her focus. Her steps faltered. She glanced at the mother of Jason's son, Rosa, who held little Jay-Jay tightly in her lap. He sat contentedly sucking his fingers. The little boy was the spitting image of his father. She felt compelled to comfort the grief-stricken woman, but the look of hatred on Rosa's face made Leah continue on to the altar. Today was not a day for a confrontation, Leah told herself.

Approaching the coffin, Leah suddenly felt the gravity of

the situation. Jason was dead. Her fingertips lightly brushed the top of the gleaming black surface. With closed eyes, she conjured up his smile. That Cheshire cat smile he gave so freely. It stole her heart and held it hostage for far too long. Nevertheless, the smooth black surface of the coffin lacked the stubble Jason sported in the morning before his shave. It lacked the wiriness of his goatee. She remembered the way his facial hair tickled her fingers, and how he would playfully try to bite her fingers for waking him. A tear escaped and ran down her cheek, quickly followed by another. "I am so sorry Jason," she whispered.

A strong arm slid around Leah's thin waist, startling her out of the private moment. "You have to go," Quincy said quietly in her ear.

"But I need to..." she began.

"I know, Leah." He gave her waist a squeeze. "I know. But Rosa..."—he looked around and dropped his voice lower— "feels you are imposing and requested that I escort you out."

Leah ran her fingers one more time over the smooth, black wood. "I don't need an escort," she said a bit too loud as it reverberated through the silence.

"I will come by later to check up on you," he said, giving her a final squeeze and turning her away from the coffin.

As Leah walked out of the sanctuary she casually tugged at the hem of her short LBD and wished it would magically grow a few more inches. Her soul felt dirty, spirit unclean. The men lusted after her, women envied her, and more often than not, she was regarded as a desperate woman who seemed to always be searching for something. Leah had tried for years to fill a bottomless pit of emptiness. Now, with Jason gone, the emptiness threatened to consume her entirely.

Chapter Two

Walking out of the church, Leah felt a renewed sense of ir-ritation and despair. The sun shone brightly in a cloudless sky and a slight breeze rustled the trees, a perfect day. How could the weather be so beautiful when she felt so awful? Footsteps emerging from the church spurred Leah across the street.

The old iron park bench looked inviting as she sank down. From there she had a clear view of the doors to the church. Mourners milled around the steps, smoking, talking, living. Her irritation inched a notch higher as she watched those people enjoying the fellowship of each other.

Fellowship. The word stomped on her nerves. One of many of the overused words rammed down her throat while growing up. The curse of being a preacher's kid, she sup-posed. Leah's formative years were lived under constant scrutiny because of her father. As a child, the congregation expected her to be a leader among her peers. Her teen years were far worse when the adults lofted the insecure girl into the role of the perfect Christian teen.

A derisive snort escaped as she remembered her mother's foreboding predictions for the unholy state of the world. How God would be coming for judgment any minute. With a shake of her head and a snap of the paper, her mother would tsk, "It's coming, mark my words; the Day of Judgment draws near!" Leah wasted many years quaking at the slightest sound, wondering if it was God descending from on high to punish her for an unholy thought.

She could not imagine worse punishments than the ones her parents doled out. Swimming was a huge no-no. It was immoral and worldly to wear a bathing suit and flaunt your body. When the opportunity presented itself, Leah jumped at the chance to sneak over to her best friend's house to go swimming. To this day, she was still not sure how she got caught, but Leah spent the next week confined to her bedroom, copying scripture passages about immorality and indecency.

Her mother always warned of God's wrath. How he would do horrible things to bring his backsliding children home. Was the recent events God's punishment, she wondered? Tears appeared unexpectedly, and rolled down her cheeks. She'd done nothing wrong by loving Jason, had she?

The physical ache in her body brought her back into the present. She was surprised to find herself sitting with her shoulders hunched forward in insecurity. It had been years since she sat like the awkward teenager she once was.

Straightening her body, Leah chanced a subtle stretch, and noticed a good-looking man heading in her direction. Several mental finger snaps clicked in her brain before she remembered his name: Calvin. He was tall, not as tall as Jason, but was a good head taller than Leah. His cool Icelandic features gave him a definitive air of chiseled masculinity.

"Hi," he said as he approached.

"Hi," she said quietly. "Nice service."

He nodded. "It was very nice."

They stared in the awkward silence for a minute or two before Calvin pointed to the bench. "Mind if I have a seat?"

Leah shook her head and slid over to make room for him.

"His life in pictures was a nice touch as well."

Leah nodded in agreement, not sure what else to say.

He finally turned to face her. "How are you holding up?"

She felt her face crumble. "I can't believe he is gone. It just doesn't seem real to me." She dabbed at her eyes and continued. "I can't believe Rosa kicked me out." She blew her nose into a Kleenex. "I am treated like the bad guy while Jason's killer roams free." She looked at Calvin. "What did Jason do to deserve this?"

Calvin shrugged. "I don't know." He ran long fingers through his light blonde hair. "And Rosa has always had a jealous streak as far as Jason is concerned." He stopped for a moment. "Was...was concerned." He settled back into the bench. "She wanted to make sure she was number one with him. There was this one time at one of the Bright Horizon games...."

"Oh that's right, you have a son who plays," Leah said, thankful to have found her footing in the conversation.

He nodded. "Tyler." His smile was friendly and infectious. "Anyway, it happened while Rosa was still pregnant with little Jay-Jay. Jason took a mother aside to speak with her, presumably about her son's emotional state during the games, but Rosa waddled her way down the bleachers and followed them into the hallway." Calvin shook his head, laughing. "Jason must have been mortified. I know I would have been with the fuss she raised and getting into that poor mother's face."

"I think I remember that or hearing about it," Leah said.

"Everyone heard of it, a classic Rosa moment." He reached out and touched Leah's shoulder with his fingers. "So please don't take her temper to heart. It isn't you, it's all her."

Both their eyes turned toward the front of the church to watch the black coffin slowly exit the building. The bright sun bounced its rays off the gleaming wood to create a halo effect around the pall bearers. They sat silently lost in thought as the coffin disappeared into the back of the hearse.

"I can't believe she made the graveside service family only."

"Just as well," Calvin said slowly. "Rosa would have thrown you in before they lowered the coffin." There was that smile again, slow and easy. "I kind of like you not covered in dirt."

Leah burst out laughing despite her bitter mood. "I suppose you're right."

They lapsed into a comfortable silence watching the hearse pull away, followed closely by the family cars. "You know," he said slowly, "I think you could use a little more levity."

"Really?" she asked, cocking an eyebrow. "What would you suggest?"

"Hockey! I have a couple tickets. My buddy Adam bailed on me this morning. Friday night. It isn't the NHL, just so you know, but the farm leagues sometimes are more entertaining."

Leah shook her head. "I'm afraid I know very little about hockey."

"Not a problem," he said, the smile back on his face. "Doesn't take long to pick up on the fundamentals, so what do you say? You want to go?"

Leah thought for a moment. Her eyes glanced toward the

church and she decided this would be the perfect way to get on with her life. "Sure, why not?" She nodded.

"Great!" he said, getting up. "I will see you Friday night." Calvin hesitated a moment. "Yep, Friday it is." He handed her a piece of paper with his telephone number and headed toward the church, chancing a glance back before he crossed the street.

Leah gave a little wave, feeling lighter than she had when she got up this morning. She collected her purse, stood, and smoothed her dress down.

After her gaze returned upward, she saw an older woman crossing the street with a younger man in tow. Leah felt a prickle of apprehension as the woman strode purposefully in her direction. Some regarded her as flashy, but Leah thought she was overly flamboyant.

Mrs. Turner wore black like the rest of the mourners, but her dress was a Michael Kors original. Her indescribable black hat would be more appropriate at a royal wedding than a funeral, and her arm candy was at least twenty years her junior.

"Leah!" she called with an arm flourish. "I am so glad I caught up with you."

She fanned her face with lace, but Leah doubted a drop of sweat could get through the multi-layers of makeup she wore.

Leah realized that she had no idea what the woman's first name was. Everyone called her Mrs. Turner. Her eyes briefly assessed the cub, her description of the arm candy, and she wondered if he called her Mrs. Turner as well. "Mrs. Turner, I was about to..."

The older woman held up a gloved hand. "I desperately need your help, Leah. With Jason's sudden death, the crowd we were expecting for the annual Bright Horizon's Charity Gala has now tripled in size. Would you be a dear and come help us make it a success?"

Leah hesitated. She wondered why this woman, who had never made a point to talk to her, suddenly needed her help.

"It's for Jason," Mrs. Turner said with an air of false sympathy.

Well that was low, Leah thought. "Sure," she said with a resigned sigh. "I have time tomorrow morning, I can stop by your office."

The skin on her cheeks pulled up to reveal her bright

white teeth. "Marvelous, see you then." She turned on her heel and marched back across the street, the man-cub trailing in her wake.

Leah wondered what she had gotten herself into. Then a secret thrill ran through her as she imagined the look on Rosa's face when she found out Leah helped with the gala.

Chapter Three

Shifting the grocery bags, Marla shook out her keys, hoping to drown out the voices behind her.

"We watched *SpongeBob* yesterday! I want *Horseland*!" Amanda argued. Marla could imagine her daughter's five-year-old face twisted in steely determination to get her way.

Tyler, at the wise old age of seven, and always trying to sound superior over his sister, answered, "*Horseland* isn't on tonight. Don't you know anything?"

Marla finally wrenched the door to the townhouse open and the children ran past her, almost knocking her over. She hauled the bags into the kitchen and hoisted them on the counter. The ache of exhaustion crept through her.

Picking up the note on the counter, Marla tried not to smirk. After nine years of marriage, this is what it came down to, a note written in orange crayon: *Went out fishing, don't bother waiting up.* She wadded the note in her hands and pitched it into the garbage.

"Kids, Daddy won't be home for dinner. What do you want? Pizza or fish sticks?" Marla called up the stairs.

Tyler's voice drifted down from his room. "I want cheese pizza."

Marla went back into the kitchen to preheat the oven. Amanda appeared with hands on hips "I want chicken nuggets."

"I didn't offer chicken nuggets, sweet pea." Marla tried to keep the weariness out of her voice. "Pizza or fish sticks?"

"Then I'm not hungry!" Folding her arms tight across her chest, Amanda stomped into the living room.

"No TV until after dinner," Marla said to the retreating

figure. "And you will get fish sticks."

She stood at the kitchen counter, took several deep breaths, and then cursed the person who first suggested breathing as a way of calming down. Her hand reached for the bottle of Xanax instead and popped a pill into her mouth. Life would be so much easier if Calvin were here with the kids. Then again, if he was home, they would pick at each other until it escalated into arguing, and the kids didn't need that. She didn't need that.

With a sigh, Marla put away the rest of the groceries and wondered where they'd gone wrong. "Nope," she said quietly. "Not going to go there."

Sliding the kids' dinner into the oven, Marla flipped through the mail. "Bills, bills, bills." She made a mental note to write a check for Tyler's little league uniform and another for Amanda's dance recital costume.

The cell phone bill seemed a bit thicker than usual. She slid her finger under the flap to open it and pulled out several sheets of paper. A gasp escaped her when she saw the total amount. It was more than double what their monthly bill averaged.

Her eyes scanned the itemized list and realized it was all on Calvin's line. His call volume had dramatically increased, including texting. Her number only popped up a couple of times on his call log. Not surprising, she mused. The only time he called her was to tell her he had picked up the kids from school.

Marla scanned the sheet a second time and found a repeat offender. The number showed up again and again, and it was called several times after nine o'clock at night and even texted after midnight. Her blood ran cold with the confirmation. She had suspected her husband was unfaithful on numerous occasions. To hold circumstantial evidence in her hands shifted the focus from possibility to probability.

She kicked the garbage can. "Fishing my ass!" she muttered, giving the can another swift kick before getting out the dinner plates. Was it the fishing that started this, she wondered? Marla had been a large supporter for his love of fishing. She knew it was his only opportunity to relax, unwind, and have time to himself. Marla had been happy for him, until she found he had cleared half their savings to purchase a new boat. That argument still rang in her ears.

Calvin tried to make amends by taking the children fishing on Saturday mornings. The peace lasted until Marla discovered he had opened a separate bank account. When confronted, he told her it was to avoid any further arguing over money, and his personal use of it.

Now, she was too tired to argue. It was easier to accept the status quo than fight for her marriage. Between her job as an accountant at a large payroll firm and raising her two kids with their activities, there was nothing left to give to her husband. Twenty-four hours in a day wasn't enough time to get it all done.

"Mom?" Tyler came into the kitchen, snapping her out of her thoughts. "I'm hungry. Is dinner ready?"

"Yes it is, little man." She tousled his blonde hair and handed him the plates. "Could you please put these on the table?"

Marla doled out fish sticks and pizza. "Amanda? Come eat some dinner."

Amanda sat in her chair and began to arrange her fish sticks by size. Marla kissed the top of her daughter's head and held her close. "I love you both very much," she said softly.

"We love you too, Mommy," Amanda answered out of the side of her mouth that wasn't smashed into her mother. "Can I eat now?"

She released her daughter to eat. "I am going to go take a quick shower. If you both finish all your dinner, you may have some ice cream for dessert." Marla pointed at her daughter. "And I will be checking the garbage, Sweet Pea."

"I wish we had a dog," Amanda sulked, taking a small bite of fish stick.

Marla tousled her sandy brown locks and headed upstairs.

Once safely hidden in her bedroom, Marla pulled the cell phone bill out and stared at it. Was he cheating on her again? She wondered. He promised never to put her through that again.

Images of a busty blonde sales clerk rose in her mind. Marla never bothered getting the specifics, like the woman's name, but Calvin had divulged some of the details during his guilt-infused confession. She ran the register at the bait and tackle shop. They met for coffee occasionally and became friends. Then he started hanging around her apartment after she broke up with her boyfriend. One thing led to another and...

Marla switched her line of thinking, not willing to relive the sordid details of his nine month affair with the bimbo. She could not bring herself to forgive him, and even went so far as to kick him out for three months. Somehow, he charmed his way back into the house.

Stripping off her clothes, she caught a glimpse of herself in the mirror. Her haggard features caught her off guard. Marla pulled at her eyes and her cheeks, wondering when she began to look so old. Was this the reason why Calvin no longer wanted her? As soon as she had the thought, she regretted it. It wasn't exactly like she rolled out the welcome mat in bed. When was the last time she had given him the opportunity to want her? With a shake of her head, Marla cleared herself of all thoughts as she headed to the shower.

Ten minutes later, she emerged clean and almost relaxed. The combination of hot water and medication gave her a nice numb feeling. Wrapping a towel around her hair and another around her body, Marla picked up the cell phone bill in one hand and the phone in the other. Taking a steadying breath, she slowly dialed the number and waited. Her heart thudded loudly in her chest; nausea rolled through her stomach.

One ring—*probably a fishing buddy,* she thought.

Two rings—*this is silly. It has to be work related,* she hoped.

Three rings—*please let me be wrong,* she prayed.

Four rings—a female voice answered with an apology that she couldn't come to the phone right now.

Chapter Four

Leah walked up to the doors of Bright Horizons and took a moment before going in. It had been awhile since she'd walked away from the company Jason built.

"Jason," she said quietly with a shake of her head. Leah attempted to conjure an image of him just beyond the doors.

"Good morning, Leah." The voice came from a tall, lanky man she recognized, but his name eluded her.

"Good morning." She mustered a smile. "How are you today?"

With a shrug the man answered, "Tutoring, coaching." He stood next to her and looked up at the stark white building. "Jason really built something special here."

Leah nodded slowly. A place to help troubled youth get back on track. That had been Jason's goal when he started Bright Horizons. She was just happy he had found a goal after the NBA decided to pass on him when he graduated from college. Leah was sure the rejection would debilitate him, but Jason was a fighter and chose to use his passion to ignite a new generation of kids who needed someone to believe in them. Keeping her tears in check, she turned to the man standing next to her.

"He certainly did," she said.

"So are you coming to work here?" His eyes looked hopeful.

Leah shook her head. "This is a one-shot deal. I'm just here to help out today."

"Well, then, welcome back," he said with a smile. "Maybe you'll change your mind?" He patted her shoulder gently and turned away.

She looked up at the building again. So many plans for this organization; most of them had come to fruition and Leah was happy to be in on the ground floor, helping Jason get started. As an event planner, she had been able to set up the first of many benefits, each becoming more popular than the previous one. Leah was happy working side by side with Jason, building a dream together. That was until Mrs. Turner became involved in the organization.

The headstrong woman had a few too many ideas and a few too many opinions. Mrs. Turner did not accept "no" as an answer.

For the sake of her sanity and relationship with Jason, Leah quit and went back to her old job shortly after Bright Horizons Youth Group became a reality and a reputable organization within the community.

With a deep, steadying breath, Leah pulled open the heavy glass doors and stepped into the cool foyer. A shiver passed over her and she wasn't sure if it was the temperature or the memory of the two officers coming to her apartment informing her of Jason's death. They questioned her whereabouts and possible motives. Although they seemed bored and disinterested with the case, Leah chose not to mention that her last conversation with Jason had ended on bittersweet terms. The nicer officer, Detective Becky, left her business card in case there was anything she remembered. It still sat on her dining room table untouched.

The front desk secretary an older woman who kept her reading glasses on a chain around her neck led Leah down the hall to an abandoned office. The small space seemed to be used as a mail room rather than an actual office. Paperwork and unopened mail littered the desk and file cabinets. The room had no décor, and was furnished sparingly. "Let me know if you need anything, I will be just up the hall." The woman smiled before leaving Leah to herself.

Leah settled herself behind a cluttered cherry wood desk and began to make mental notes as she situated herself. The message light on the answering machine was blinking rapidly. Leah frowned, wondering when the last time someone had checked the voicemail. She reached for it and stopped. Her hand hung in midair, hovering over the small silver box. What if one of the messages was from Jason? How would she handle that? The next thought was one of chastisement as she firmly pushed the play button.

First rule of event planning: one small detail gone wrong would cause a ripple of chaos that could bring an entire event to a screeching halt. *Leave nothing to chance, not even at the possibility of hearing a dead lover's voice on an answering machine.*

Her hand flew quickly over the pad of paper. The catering company needed confirmation of a liquor license. The DJ needed confirmation of set up time. The venue needed confirmation of the liquor license. The photographer never received the check for the deposit. When all the messages played through, she continued scrawling as if she were still taking dictation. *Finalize the VIP list, send it to the security team, and check with the florist—just to be safe, call health inspector—cover all bases.*

A soft knock on the door did not stem the scrawling of note taking. "Yes?" she said, without looking up.

The person who knocked entered the small office. "Leah? I know you're crunched for time, but I need to have a talk with you." He continued to stand and reached for a couple of sugar cookies on a silver platter.

She recognized the voice and said, "Tanvir, I don't know how old those are." Still not looking up, she continued, "Looks like no one has been in to clean this office in awhile."

Tanvir spit the cookie into what she assumed was a handkerchief after she heard him pull something out of the breast pocket of his sports coat. "You could have warned me."

"That would not have been half as much fun." She smiled, looking up from her list for the first time. The man in front of her was not as tall as the typical basketball player, but he made up for the height difference with a smug, self-assured confidence that could rattle some people's nerves. His clipped English accent only accentuated his assumed arrogance, but Leah knew better. She knew Tanvir put his heart and soul into this operation and believed in it almost as much as Jason did.

"What did you need, Tanvir?"

Discreetly wiping at his tongue with his handkerchief, he smoothed down his linen sport coat before answering. "I have been going over the company budget and I can't seem to access all the files. Did Jason say anything about changing passwords to you?"

Leah shook her head slowly. That made no sense, she thought. Jason always rotated the same three passwords because he could not stand trying to remember useless information. Tanvir, being one of Jason's best friends and right hand financial man, would know this fact as well.

"We were in the process of acquiring a new company van," Tanvir continued. "Jason and I had mapped out a budget for the rest of the year, but when I called Mike at the loan office to fax over the paperwork, he informed me he was not able to do so."

Leah's stomach began to churn with apprehension. This did not bode well. Even though no one had met with Jason's estate attorney, it was a given that Tanvir would automatically take the financial reigns of the organization. He had been at the financial helm from the start.

He sat heavily in a chair across from her. "From what I can gather, the Turners have co-ownership over Bright Horizons. The paperwork was already faxed over to Mrs. Turner in regard to our financing."

Leah chewed on her bottom lip, wondering how much she should say about Jason leaving the company to the Turners. It was Mrs. Turner's brother, the mayor himself, who initially invested in Jason's dream. In an attempt to honor the dead, Leah decided to err on the side of keeping out of it.

"You know what I would love?" she said suddenly.

His eyes narrowed. "What?"

"I miss our backgammon lunches; do you still have your board?"

"Yes?" He sounded a bit hesitant.

Leah tried to keep her voice light, happy. "Let's go to the sandwich shop around the corner, my treat, play some backgammon. I will need something to look forward to after I make this round of phone calls."

He glanced at her growing list. "Esh, I do not envy you." A smile finally emerged. "Okay, I will pick you up here at one o'clock, and I will only allow you to pay because those are the set rules, loser picks up the tab."

"Well then, maybe we should just wait and see." She returned his smile, picking up the phone.

Tanvir walked out of the office, shaking his head. "I forgot how utterly delusional you are. It will be nice to defeat you again, my friend."

Leah was on an endless loop in Calvin's mind. He could hardly wait for their date tonight. Just the thought of being with her gave him a flutter of excitement.

Turning onto the street where he lived, his thoughts shifted from excitement to apprehension. He never imagined that being married could be so hard; it was obvious they were both unhappy, as if two strangers were living in the same house, trying to raise a family.

He wondered briefly if she had found out about Vivian and then quickly rejected the idea. There was no way for Marla to know. Vivian had been a mistake, a very brief mistake that he had remedied quickly. The affair escalated too quickly, she didn't understand boundaries, called a little too often, and became a little too needy.

The soft crunch he heard pulling into the driveway made him curse. Climbing out of his Yukon Denali, Calvin crouched down to see the bent handlebars of his son's bike. Pulling the bicycle out of the way, Calvin put it in the garage and decided to replace it only if Tyler brought home a decent report card.

Walking in the front door, the heavenly aroma of pot roast surrounded him. He followed the scent into the kitchen. Marla was putting dinner rolls into the oven. "It's Friday night. What are you doing cooking on a Friday night?" he asked slowly, a bit on the wary side.

"I thought we could do something different tonight." She straightened, offering him a smile. First smile she gave him in weeks. "Have a nice dinner; watch a movie with the kids." Her eyes looked a bit hopeful.

"That sounds great," he said hesitantly, "but I have plans after dinner." The small shift of emotion in her face brought a lie quickly to his lips. "There's a big poker tournament tonight," he said impulsively. "I won't be out late." He headed down the hall calling over his shoulder, "And I'm taking the kids fishing in the morning."

Calvin slid open the closet door and began to thumb through his wardrobe. *What to wear?* he asked himself. A bright pink bag on the floor caught his eye. He pulled the white flimsy negligee out very slowly, trying to figure out what it was doing in the closet. He held it up between his two hands and imagined the white silk and lace hugging Leah's curves. A surge of guilt coursed through him as he realized his *wife* had bought this for him—for them.

The delicate material was dropped back into the pink bag quickly, as if his fingers had been burned. Did Marla actually want to work on this marriage? Did she think this would fix them? They had separated once, but he hadn't been ready to give up on his family and begged Marla for a second chance. His wife's voice calling out dinner pulled him back into the present. Back to the family he'd pleaded to be with, but hadn't been very faithful to.

Calvin jumped in the shower after dinner, calculating his time and driving distance. He didn't want to be late to pick up Leah. His stomach jolted as he thought of her smile, the way she tilted her head when she spoke. Wrapped in his thoughts, he didn't notice his wife leaning against the wall until the shower was over and he slid the shower door open.

"Oh God! Marla." He clutched his chest. "Say something next time." He laughed nervously, thankful he didn't let his thoughts wander too far during his shower.

"Sorry, Cal." Marla handed him a towel. "You know,"— she took a step closer to him—"I can have Janice watch the kids...." There was that slightly hopeful expression again. "I can go with you."

Drying off quickly, he tried to assuage his own guilt. She was attempting to breathe life into a dying relationship, and he was feeling like a nervous teenager getting ready for prom.

"Look," he said, hoping his voice sounded flat and even, "I won't be out long." A shirt went over his head. "Just a couple of rounds of poker with the guys, I promise." He pulled on his jeans. "Besides,"—he cupped her cheek in his hand—"you look tired. Maybe you should get some rest."

Leah sat on the sofa, determined not to look at her watch. Her foot shook with nervous anticipation as she thumbed through a magazine. "Get a grip, Leah," she said quietly. The jarring sound of the doorbell caused her to jump off the couch. She laughed at her anxious reaction. A steady hand reached for the doorknob.

"Hi!" Calvin smiled.

"Hi," she said, stepping aside. He handed her a large brown bag as he brushed past her. "This is for you and you are not allowed to open it until we get to the game."

Leah looked at the plain bag decorated with stickers and tied with a ribbon. "Um, okay..."

He shrugged. "I didn't want to bring flowers. I wanted you to remember this."

She found his slight nervous tension charming. "I don't think I will have a problem remembering this." Her laugh was small. "This will be my first hockey game."

Calvin's eyes bulged. "Your first? You've never..."

With a slow shake of her head, Leah said, "I told you I know very little about the game."

He offered his arm. "Well then, we had better get you educated!"

The decorated bag swung awkwardly in her hand as she locked the door behind her. "Sure I can't just take a little peek?"

"Nope," Calvin answered quickly. "I picked that up as a special gift for you. You need to have your own..." He stopped mid-sentence. Leah assumed it was to keep from giving away the surprise.

"Okay." She smiled, taking his arm once again. Leah was amazed that he opened the car door for her and could not remember the last time a man had done that. "Thank you," she murmured, climbing into the Yukon. She loved how the soft leather seats molded around her, cradling her body. "This is a nice car," she said, buckling her seatbelt.

"I like it." He turned the key and eased out of the parking lot. "I hope you're hungry. The Poplar Ice Center has an amazing restaurant."

"Do we have time before the game?" She glanced at her watch.

"We can eat during the game. It's like having box seats."

"Wow, so it's kind of like dinner theater?"

Calvin laughed aloud. "Kind of, I guess. I would never have compared the two."

"Jason and I went to a dinner theater once. It made me too uncomfortable, eating while people were performing." She suppressed the urge to shiver. "I imagine, though, with all the action on the ice, my chewing will not bother the players?"

"Probably not." He shook his head.

Leah embraced the silence that lingered in the car. She chanced a look at Calvin. He seemed sweet and was definitely charming. This was already the most memorable first date she has been on and it hadn't even started yet. Despite all her mental debates and warnings, she found herself attracted to the man. Leah had to remind herself that she would be going slowly. No need risking her heart again.

"I always thought Jason was too arrogant and stubborn to settle down," he said lightly. "You could do so much better than him."

After a couple minutes of shocked silence, Leah was able to find her voice. "I agree," she said slowly, not ready to talk about her complicated relationship with Jason. She barely understood the intricate wiring of the connection they shared. How could she discuss it with a semi-stranger?

"Oh, I am sorry," he said, pulling into the parking garage. "I really shouldn't have." Quickly parking the car in the first available spot, he turned to look at Leah. "I should have just kept my opinions to myself."

"It's alright, Calvin." She rested her hand on his forearm. "You have your opinions, and you are entitled to them."

Their eyes remained locked. She could feel the energy building between them and realized her resolve would be short-lived staring into his ice blue eyes. Thankfully, he turned away first. Quickly exiting the car, he hurried over to her side before she could figure out how to open the door.

"Thank you," she giggled, taking his hand to exit the car.

Once she was on the ground, she didn't release his hand and he didn't let go. They walked hand in hand into the Poplar Ice Center.

"Oh my gosh!" She bit into her salad and tried not to roll her eyes in delight. "This dressing has got to be close to a thousand calories. It's too good."

The ice bunnies had just taken the court to cheer on the home team. Calvin was not exaggerating about the bird's-eye-view seating. The restaurant surrounded half the rink like a giant horseshoe.

The crowd went wild as the home team took the ice. Whistles, air horns, and megaphones shook the rafters. Black pucks bounced off the glass walls. Leah's eyes went wide. "I had no idea that hockey could be so exciting?"

He shook his head with a smile. "It is more fun once the game gets started." His eyes slid to the brown paper bag.

"Can I open it now?"

He nodded, a secret smile playing about his kissable lips. Leah struck the thought as soon as she had it, reminding herself that she was going to go slow. Her fingers untied the ribbon, opened the bag, and pulled out a hot pink, plastic blow horn with her name written across the side in silver sparkle letters. She held his gift in her hands, not sure how to respond.

"It's to cheer the team on," he said with a bit of embarrassment. "The point of coming to the games is to have fun and be loud and obnoxious." She could feel Calvin watching her. "You don't have to use it," he said quickly. "It really was a silly thought."

Before she could remember the words dignity and decorum, Leah stood up, leaned over the glass wall, and blew into her horn as hard as she could. The loud blast echoed around the auditorium and several people looked in her direction. Pulling herself back into the restaurant, she cocked an eyebrow. "Like that?" she asked.

Calvin nodded. "I would say you're a natural," he said, laughing.

Leah sat down and scooted back up to the table. "I think I might enjoy hockey after all."

"Yeah?" His eyes lowered into a sly stare. "Care to make a wager?"

"Sure." Leah liked the ease of being with Calvin. "What are the stakes?"

"If the home team makes the first goal, I get a kiss."

Her heart beat a little faster, but she kept her voice even. "And if the opposing team scores first?"

He gave a non-committal shrug. "Then you can kiss me."

"That hardly seems like a fair trade," she said. *But I'm game,* she added silently.

His face was a mass of playful shrewdness. "Then what do you want?"

Oh, the possibilities. "I get to choose the next date," she said, extending her hand.

He sat for a moment longer. The opening buzzer sounded,

voices, scuffling, and ice clinking rose up from the floor. Slowly, his hand reached across the table, grasping hers. "Deal," he said.

The announcer screamed, "G-O-A-L!" stretching out every letter, ensuring one little word reverberated throughout the ice center.

Leah felt as surprised as Calvin looked. "Is that normal?" she asked loudly over the noise. "A goal at the opening shot?"

They both rose and looked down onto the ice, then up to the scoreboard. The glaring red 00 of the home team clicked up 01.

"No, it isn't normal, but it isn't unheard of." His slow smile spread. "I am a little disappointed. I was really looking forward to a second date."

Leah's heart fluttered a little faster. Being with him, wanting him, felt so right, so natural—it was too easy. Something had to go wrong.

Calvin leaned closer. "But not that disappointed," he said as their lips met.

Leah stood in the middle of her living room rethinking her cleaning plan. Piles of books surrounded her, and she felt a bit overwhelmed looking at the empty bookcases lining the wall. Organization had always been her strong suit until the fall out with Jason. Leah felt she could barely function.

As the array of clutter closed in around her, a single clear thought emerged through the chaos...*move*. Leah took a moment to savor the thought. What was keeping her there? Jason was gone, there was no family nearby, not that she would want to live near her family. The very thought made her shudder. The pink, sparkled blow horn caught her eye. Calvin. She'd had a good time on their date, and there was potential for something, but was it enough to hang around? Why stay? Her lease was up in a couple of months.

The thought of moving actually made her a bit giddy. The possibilities were endless. Where would she go? For the first time, she felt she had the world at her feet and the ability to see it all. Grabbing an atlas from one of the book piles, she moved another pile off the sofa to sit down. Leah thumbed through, carefully weighing each state before she realized she was being silly.

As she stood up, a photograph fluttered out of the pages. Leah picked it up and looked at it. Tears began to form as she lingered over the two smiling faces in the picture. It was hard to believe they were once so incredibly happy. Had they ever been that happy? That content? Leah wondered why she'd waited around for so long. She would still be waiting if he were still alive.

Through the arguments and the tears, Leah was willing to

stand by Jason. To accept his son, weather through the drama with Rosa, and build his dream together. A little voice in the back of her head asked, *"What about your dream?"*

"My dream?" she said aloud. It had been so long since she'd thought about what she wanted. Looking at the picture again, she couldn't help but remember how encouraging Jason was that she pursue her "dream..."

The lounge was almost empty except for a couple in a darkened corner and someone sitting at the bar. "Someone told me about this place," Jason said. "The music is supposed to be lively and entertaining."

They both eyed the lonely piano in the middle of the room. "Looks like the pianist took the night off," Leah said, running her fingers over the gleaming wood.

"Can I get you folks anything to drink?" the server asked.

"I think I'll just have an iced tea," Leah said, her eyes lingering on the keys. Her fingers itched to tap out some notes.

She heard Jason order a beer and saw him slide onto the bench. He awkwardly tapped out 'Mary had a Little Lamb.' With a shy shrug, he said, "I've always wanted to learn, but Dad thought basketball was more practical." And there was the grin, his special smile that made her heart race and melt all at the same time. Leah was sure that if he gave her that smile, she would do anything he asked, no matter how illegal or depraved it might be. "You play?"

She nodded slowly. "A little." Her feet remained rooted to the spot.

He tapped out a few more clunky notes and patted the seat beside him. "Anything has got to be better than what I am doing."

Hesitantly, she approached the bench and sat down next to him.

"Can you play chopsticks?" he asked, pounding out the notes. His finger position was off and the melody sounded broken.

She took hold of his hand. "I can play chopsticks." She nodded, lightly touching a key. The clink of the A hung in the air for a moment before she followed it with two more notes.

Out of the corner of her eye, she saw Jason's eyes glimmer. "How much do you play?"

Before she could stop, her fingers began to fly across the keyboard, playing one of the old spiritual hymns she grew up with. "I started dabbling when I was three. My grandparents had an old upright. I used to love playing it." Her fingers flew confidently over the keys.

Jason rose and leaned against the side, listening to her story.

She slipped into another song and continued without missing a single note. "Before long, I was able to pick up the music by ear and played the piano at the weekly church services for my father."

"Why didn't you do something with this?"

Leah shrugged, moving into a more difficult Chopin piece. "My mother said that it was God's gift and not to be squandered anywhere other than church." She felt free when she played. The music moved all the bad feelings away and replaced it with an inner peace she longed for.

"So like your father, my mother felt that my time should be spent concentrating on a more practical career." Leah kept her mother's advice to herself. "Young ladies are expected to do ungodly things to advance in the music industry. You'd best steer clear. Keep your soul pure."

She shifted easily into Mozart, and Jason shook his head. "Don't you need sheet music to do this?"

Her laugh mingled perfectly with the music. "No, my grandmother always said, 'A good pianist doesn't need sheets of notes; they can feel the music flow freely through their fingertips.'"

Jason sat down and grabbed Leah's hands. The abruptness of silence surprised her. "You need to pursue this, you can play!"

Leah shook her head. "No, Jason, I gave up on ever being a pianist." She nodded her head slowly, trying to keep her tears in check. "I have reconciled with the fact that..."

"Well, I haven't," he said a little too loudly. Looking around, he dropped his voice a notch. "You are very talented and I can see a very bright future for you as a pianist...

The jarring ring of the telephone pulled Leah back into the present. It took her a couple of rings to find the buried cell phone. "Hello?"

"Hey, Leah, it's Quincy. I was just calling to check up on you."

She settled back into a small section of the couch. "Hi, Quincy. I'm doing okay."

"You sure?" She could hear the concern in his voice. "You sound a little sad."

The picture of her and Jason crumpled in her fist. "Well, you know how it is. I'm surrounded by ghosts at every turn." Her inner voice urged her to change the subject quickly. "How are you doing?"

"Well, that kind of brings me to the second purpose of this call. Would you mind coming in this afternoon? There is still so much to do for the gala, and we can use all the help we can get."

Leah looked at her watch, then at the mess in her living room. "Yep, I can be there in a couple of hours."

Saying her goodbyes, Leah hung up the phone and made a mental note to pick up, packing boxes along the way. When her lease was up, she was moving to her neon oasis—Las Vegas. Leah was going to be a pianist.

Running thirty minutes late, Leah pulled into the parking lot of Bright Horizons Youth Group. She didn't see Mrs. Turner and Rosa until she almost collided into them.

"Oh, oops, sorry," Leah said, fumbling with her purse and notebook. "I, um, didn't see you there." The look on Rosa's face was pure anger.

"Well, we are certainly glad you're here," Mrs. Turner said with an airy smile. "There is just so much that needs to be done, and well, it is your business to know how to do this."

Leah smiled, situating her purse on her shoulder, and avoided eye contact with Rosa in case one of the thousand daggers thrown from her eyes would penetrate. "You know, I am just happy to help," she said to the older woman. Leah cringed at the overly eager sound of her own voice.

"And we are so glad you are helping, swallowing your pride for the good of Bright Horizons." Mrs. Turner wore her Armani dress like it was a second skin, her makeup and hair flawless as always. Her smile was etched, and didn't quite spread to the rest of her face.

"I don't understand why..." Rosa said. Her hostility spoke volumes.

Leah braced herself for a very vocal confrontation.

"No, dear." Mrs. Turner put a beautifully manicured hand on Rosa's forearm. "You don't understand, and you never will if you don't check your attitude."

A car horn caused all three women to look around. "Ah, that's for me." Mrs. Turner pulled a sheet of paper from her book, not acknowledging the impatient student honking.

Leah didn't want to know why the University's current basketball star was sitting in Mrs. Turner's car.

"If you both will excuse me, I have more important matters to attend to." She handed Leah a long list, "Be a dear and see if you can crank this out."

The two women eyed each other warily.

Rosa brushed past Leah. "Don't you dare screw this up," she hissed.

"Why would you think that?" Leah usually kept to herself as far as Rosa was concerned, but the implication bothered her.

Rosa slid on a pair of sunglasses. "Because you screw everything up."

🎹

Tiptoeing quietly into her son's room, Rosa pulled the Scooby Doo blanket up over his shoulders. Moving a lock of hair across his forehead, her fingers trailed down his cheek. It hit her, as it always did, how much he looked like Jason. Rosa could feel her heart contract as the anger started to simmer.

Straightening up, Rosa wandered over to the window. Outside was dark and calm. If she cocked her head just right, she could see some stars in the blue velvet sky, but she didn't want to look for the stars tonight. Leah had disrupted her afternoon and ruined her mood for the rest of the evening. Standing on the Bright Horizon steps, looking long and lean with her cute little outfit and big doe eyes.

Rosa pulled her sweater tight across her ample chest and stewed—stewed over everything that Leah had taken from her, everything that Jason had given willingly to her and not to Rosa.

Little Jay-Jay stirred in his sleep. Rosa looked at him and felt a pang of guilt as her anger rose a couple of degrees higher. Maybe trapping Jason into a relationship with the baby wasn't the greatest idea in the world. She did threaten to leave once and take their son far away, but Jason gave that stupid smile that made her blood boil because she knew, as did he, that she needed him.

All Leah had to do was call crying and he scrambled to get to her. Rosa followed him one night after a mysterious phone call. He told her it was Tanvir on the phone and that he would be back in a few. As soon as his headlights disappeared down the street, she packed up their son and followed him all the way to Leah's apartment where he stayed for three hours.

She confronted him when he got home. Jason swore they weren't intimate that evening and that he had gone over to comfort her. There was some argument with her mother or something stupid like that.

Rosa believed him, but then reluctantly admitted to herself she wished it had been sexual. Jason dropped all his plans for the evening to comfort Leah. Rosa's anger rose even higher as she realized she was the burden, and Leah was the special one.

Women came and went from Jason's life, all clamoring for attention. Leah never had to try. There was a special place in his heart for her and Rosa was just there to be appeased.

"Guess you can't appease me anymore," she said quietly in the darkness. "You got *exactly* what you deserved, Jason Rowe."

Chapter Six

Leah shuffled through a mountain of papers. "Where is it?" she muttered, shifting through another sheaf piled high on the desk. "It has got to be here somewhere." As she reached for a third stack, her hands froze in mid air. When had this happened? She wondered to herself. Didn't she quit this job? Stepping away from the desk, Leah tried to calm the thudding of her heart. She was sure the guest list was around the office somewhere. Maybe Tanvir took it. She made a mental note to ask him when he got back from his unexplained errand.

Walking into the hall, the oppressive weight of the office began to lighten and the urge to use the restroom replaced it. The vending machine was across the way. As tempting as a Snickers bar sounded, Leah opted for using the washroom instead. She would treat herself to a decent meal once she got a little more work done.

Arriving at the restroom, Leah saw that the door to Jason's office was ajar. Something didn't seem right, but after a moment of mental debate, Leah decided to mind her own business. As she left the bathroom, however, she heard rustling and a light *clink*, as if something was knocked over. She stood beside the doorway for a moment listening to the shuffling of papers.

Flashes of horror movies ran through her head. After all, Jason's killer was still on the loose, she reasoned. Leah's imagination ran wild; her eyes darted down the hall, wondering if she had time to run back to her office to call the police. The rustling in the office stopped, followed by an eerie silence.

With a silent count to ten, Leah slowly opened the door wider to find the room empty of any knife-wielding lunatics.

This had been the first time stepping in here since Jason's death. It was a bit surreal, being in his personal space. Everything looked as if he just stepped away and would be back any moment. The flood of emotions was unexpected, so many conversations surrounded by those four walls.

His bookcase was filled with an eclectic assortment of books, knickknacks, and a small conch shell. Leah picked up the shell, held it to her ear, and could hear the roar of the ocean. Placing the shell back onto the ledge, she noticed a folder sitting a shelf higher, cocked at an odd angle. Curiosity got the better of her as she pulled it down. Before she could flip it open, pain shot through the back of her head and everything went black.

Pacing the dock for a half an hour, Leah's demeanor went from mild irritation to blood-boiling anger. Bouncing her cell in between her fingers, she checked it every few seconds to see if she had missed a message from Jason canceling their date or an explanation for his tardiness. The yacht was due to set sail in less than ten minutes. She watched the other couples laughing, talking, and kissing. She felt a pang of jealousy. Jason was very reserved with his affection. He never introduced her as his girlfriend and never held her hand in public.

His tall frame broke into her line of sight and all sense of anger fled as she rushed into his arms. Jason laughed, returning the embrace briefly before distancing himself. "What was that for?" he asked. His smile had dimmed lightly.

"I'm just glad you're here," she said, her smile doubling in wattage.

As the couple boarded the yacht, Leah admired the lavish decorations surrounding her. The maitre d' greeted them with a pleasant nod. "Mr. Rowe, it is a pleasure to have you and your lady friend as our guest tonight." Jason smiled. "Well I'm glad you didn't set sail without us." They were led to a candle-lit table next to a window that overlooked the water. Within minutes a server approached with a bottle of Krug Clos d'Ambonnay. "Care to try our most exclusive bottle, a 1995 first edition." Leah heard Jason thank the man as he filled each of their glasses before leaving them to talk.

They shared a romantic meal in an elegant dining room. The string quartet set the mood as they sipped champagne and talked easily.

An older gentleman approached their table. "Take your picture?" he asked, holding up his camera.

"Oh yes," Leah answered quickly, getting up.

"Wait?" Jason said, watching her. "What are you doing?"

"Getting closer, silly." She settled herself on his lap.

His discomfort was lost on her. "Do you have to sit on my lap, Leah?"

She put her arm around his neck. "Where do you suggest I sit? Across the table where I was?" Pulling his face close to hers, she smiled pretty for the camera.

"Oh that is beautiful, you make a lovely couple." The photographer smiled graciously, his eyes downcast. "Is this yours?" He picked up the conch shell.

"No." Jason held up his hands, shifting to get Leah off his lap. "Doesn't belong to us."

The photographer turned the shell over in his hands. "It is a beautiful piece of nature. Maybe you should just keep it here." He placed it on the table. "In case someone comes looking for it."

"Why would anyone want a shell?" Jason picked it up and handed it over to Leah.

She marveled at the contrast between smooth and rough. "We will take good care of it." She nodded to the photographer.

He moved on to another table, leaving them to discuss the piece of nature that sat in front of them. As they debated exactly what a conch was, Jason pointed to the photographer behind Leah. She turned and watched him pull an identical conch shell out from under the table of another couple.

"I think we've been swindled," Jason laughed.

Leah joined in. "I only think it is considered swindled if we gave him money."

The quartet started a slow romantic tune. "Would you like to dance?"

He led Leah to the dance floor and she fell into his arms. As they swayed in time to the music, Leah prayed that night would never end.

Back on dry land, it was business as usual. Jason maintained a reasonable distance as he escorted Leah to his SUV. Although the conversation continued, Leah could tell something was on Jason's mind as they headed back to his house.

The ringing of his cell phone set her teeth on edge. Leah

could tell by the way he answered that it was a woman. He spoke briefly and hung up. "Sorry, Leah," he said. Finding an opening in traffic, he made a wide U-turn. "We are going to have to cut this evening short."

"Why?" She asked, trying to keep the suspicion out of her voice. "What's up?"

"Work stuff." He kept his eyes glued to the road. "Tanvir is having an inverting problem."

"Oh well, if that's all, I can go back to the office with you. Maybe I can help."

"No," he cut her off quickly. "I'm not going to subject you to the boredom."

There were several faces hovering around Leah as she came to, but only two were recognizable.

"Hey," Quincy said, his face twisted with worry and stress.

Pain throbbed through Leah's skull. "Oh, Quincy. What happened?" she asked quietly.

"We were hoping you could tell us." The nice officer, Detective Becky, squatted down next to her. "Do you remember anything about the attack?"

Her hand slowly patted the back of her head; the giant goose egg sitting at the base of her skull made her feel faint. "No." Her breathless voice was barely audible. "No, I don't know who attacked me."

"It probably was one of the troublemakers hanging around," the less sympathetic cop said without looking down at Leah.

Quincy shook his head. "Our boys wouldn't do something like this."

Leah heard Mrs. Turner's voice cut through the ringing in her ears. "I'll get you a list of our most troubled kids." She rounded the desk and looked down at Leah. "Go home, Leah. You've done enough for this organization. We don't need any more negative publicity, thank you."

The nice officer smiled. "In case you didn't keep my information." She offered a plain white card with raised black lettering. "Detective Becky Melbourne, Homicide." Folding the card into Leah's hand, she gave it a pat. "Call me if you need anything, okay?"

Leah nodded slowly, but the pain in her head hurt too much. If she was attacked, Leah wondered if it was the same person who killed Jason. Her head spun with questions.

Snuggling down into the couch, Leah flipped through a hundred channels before finding a Harrison Ford movie she had never seen. Before she could get too involved with the plot, her phone rang.

The caller ID let Leah know it was her mother. With a heavy sigh, she answered the phone, knowing if she didn't, her mother would show up unannounced on her doorstep.

"Leah?" her mother began before Leah could say hello. "Are you all right?"

"Yes, Mother," she responded dutifully. "I am fine, how are you?"

"Someone from Bright Horizons called saying you had been attacked. Is that true?" Her mother's clipped voice sounded more terse than usual.

The urge to roll her eyes was intense. The pain it caused was as well. "Yes, Mother, it is true. I was attacked this afternoon, but I am fine."

She heard the sanctimonious scoff through the phone line. "Evil begets evil, Leah. When you associate with evildoers..."

"Yes, Mother, I know." She chanced a sigh. Normally, she would just let her mother rant, but Leah didn't think her head could withstand a 90-minute sermon. "Lie down with dogs and I'm covered in fleas."

"Leah," she scolded, "I knew this worldly behavior would turn you away from God's plan. Honor thy father and mother. Turn your back on the ways of the world, Leah. The Day of Judgment is at hand..."

"Oh Mother, I have to go. It is time for my medication. Thanks for calling." Leah quickly hung up the phone. She knew that the disrespectful attitude was asking for trouble, but she really was not in the mood for the religious onslaught. The phone rang in her hand. It was her mother again. She turned the ringer to silent and sank back down into the sofa.

A loud knock on the door caused her to jump. Leah tiptoed to the peephole and held her breath. She opened the door to a smiling Calvin.

"What are you doing here?" she asked, discreetly combing the back of her dark hair down with her fingers.

"I heard about what happened," he said, walking in without invitation. "And brought you some dinner from Angelo's." Calvin headed to the kitchen, calling over his shoulder, "Hope you like pasta."

She followed the smell of garlic and marinara. Her stomach gave a loud growl of approval. "How did you find out about what happened?"

He took down a couple of plates and hunted for forks. "There was a blurb on the news."

Leah took two forks from the dish drainer and headed to the table. "It made the news?"

"There was a small segment on the news about the attack and that the police had no leads." He brought the plates and food over. "So what happened?"

With a shrug, Leah dished out some ravioli. "I was looking at Jason's bookshelf, and then I was looking up at Quincy."

"Quincy? Why Quincy?"

"From what I can gather, he was the one who found me and called nine-one-one." She unwrapped the garlic bread and put a couple slices on his plate. "You okay?" she asked. His face had hardened a little

"I'm fine." He poured some bottled water into two wine goblets. "I assumed you'd be on medication." He laughed. "I figured water was a safe bet. So you didn't see who attacked you?"

She shook her head. "Nope." Taking a bite of ravioli, she closed her eyes. "I had no idea how hungry I was until right this second." Her petite hand covered Calvin's large one sitting on the table. "Thank you. This was very thoughtful of you."

Lifting his free hand, he caressed her cheek briefly before turning back to the meal. "Well I know you had a hard day. Mine was just as long and I didn't get any lunch." He pulled out a box. "And I knew you weren't feeling well. So I got you a little something to make you smile."

With a little flutter of anticipation, Leah took the box. "Calvin you really shouldn't have."

"It really isn't much."

Lifting the lid off the box, Leah couldn't help but laugh even with the pounding in her head. She lifted a bright yellow ice bag out of the box. The big black smiley face made her laugh harder. "I love it, Calvin, thank you so much!" Gathering him in a hug, she kissed his cheek. "This is so sweet of you."

Together, they spent a leisurely evening snuggling on the couch watching TV and chatting. When it was time to say goodbye, Leah felt a little sad to watch him go and a little irritated at her growing attraction for him.

Her stomach did a small flip when he sent her a text five minutes after their goodbyes.

I really like spending time with you.

Her stomach flipped again. *I do too.*

Would love to watch the sunset with you on my boat.

Her thumbs flew over the keypad. *Let me know when and where.*

I will. Sleep well, sweet Leah.

Chapter Seven

Children ran wild, screaming and playing in the backyard. Marla sipped on her drink slowly, hoping the ice in her glass would squelch the heat of anger and embarrassment rising within her. Calvin had stood her up again. Before she could mask her emotions, her friend Sylvia sat down beside her with two plates in her hands. "Great party," Marla said, taking another sip.

"Any party involving cake is a good one." She handed Marla a slice of vanilla sponge cake covered in icing. "Saved you a piece."

Marla eyed the dismembered dessert across the yard. "I think there will be plenty of leftovers." Taking the cake, she balanced it on her knee. She knew she shouldn't eat the calorie ridden food. It had taken her forever to struggle into her jeans this morning.

Eyeing the hostess across the way, Marla felt inferior and wondered what Janice did differently. Janice had a nice body, perfect skin, and an attentive husband who adored her. Marla watched Glen, her husband, take a break from throwing the football with the older kids to check on his wife. He lovingly placed a kiss on Janice's forehead, and said something in her ear to make her laugh.

With four children, where were the bags under *her* eyes? Where was the 'what am I doing here?' expression that Marla was sure haunted her own face every single day? Janice had it so together, Marla felt as if she had to be doing something wrong.

Oh, and the upbeat personality. *Let's not forget that,* Marla thought wryly.

"You okay?" Sylvia asked.

Marla gestured with her fork. "Janice and Glen are irritating me."

"Why?" Sylvia asked with surprise.

"It's a children's birthday party. Shouldn't they tone it down a bit?"

Her friend laughed. "I think holding hands is tame enough. These children are not in danger of sexual corruption." She took a bite of cake. "What's with the mood?"

"What mood?" Marla attempted a bite of cake. It felt as if she were chewing sawdust. "I don't feel like watching all this gooey, lovey-dovey nonsense. Janice looks like a love struck teenager."

"I think it's sweet." Sylvia took another bite. "After fifteen years of marriage, Janice and Mark act as if they are still on their first date."

"What makes them so special?" Marla grumbled, stabbing at her dessert.

"Ah, I get it now." She nodded. "This isn't about a good marriage; this is about one that's not so good."

Setting the plate aside, Marla sipped on her drink. "I don't know what you're talking about."

"Sure I do. Why not talk to me?" Sylvia looked around. "Where is Calvin anyway? Maybe the two of you should..."

"Calvin's not here," Marla said quietly. "He had something better to do than spend time with his family."

Sylvia slid an arm through Marla's and nudged her with a shoulder. "Things still haven't gotten better since he begged you to come home?"

"Nope." Marla swayed her head from side to side. "He treats our home as a stop-over station in between poker games, fishing trips, and who knows what else."

The silence stretched between them. Marla broke first. "I tried to make it work, but it feels like I am the only one fighting for this." She kept her tears in check. Marla didn't want her children to see her crying.

"What are you going to do?" Sylvia asked quietly.

Marla squeezed her friend's hand, "Soon as he gets home tonight, I am asking him to move out. Life is too short to be this miserable."

Leah jiggled her foot nervously as she waited for someone to answer the other end of her phone call.

"Hello?"

"Quincy, hi! It's Leah."

"Hi, Leah, how are you feeling today?"

"Better, better, thanks." She took a deep breath, bracing
herself before saying her crazy idea out loud. "I wanted to
talk to you, about, um." Leah began to pace. "Okay..." She
took a deep breath. This was crazy.

"Are you all right?"

"Me? Oh, I'm fine," she said, taking another breath. "There
is an open audition in Vegas for pianists and I am one, a pianist, I mean." The words tumbled from her mouth quickly. "I've
played most of my life and am thinking of going...to Vegas...to
audition." She could feel the excitement bubbling up. "I have
always wanted to play professionally, but was talked into a
more practical career. I know this is a major life change and
needed to talk about it, with someone."

"Vegas?" he asked.

Leah's head bounced. "Vegas. I have always loved Vegas,
the bright, flashing neon, the pulsing beat of the city."

Quincy laughed. "That's the thump of the slots you feel."

"Seriously! I am actually considering this and would like
an unbiased opinion."

"What are the auditions for?"

"A brand new stage show for..." She scanned the article
again. "Doesn't say who."

"Well, if you want my honest opinion."

Leah sunk down onto a dining room chair. "You know I
do." She braced for the worst.

"Follow your dream, Leah. If that is where your heart
lies, you need to do it now."

"Really?"

"Hey, all I've ever wanted to do was play basketball. When
I didn't get picked up by the NBA, I went the international
route. Of course I am kind of in a free agent limbo right now,
but I am helping others here at Bright Horizons until I get
picked up again."

"How are things going over there?"

"Not near as exciting since you've been gone. No one has been knocked unconscious or maimed."

Leah laughed softly. "I have to get going. I have a date in a bit."

"Oh?" His voice rose in surprise. "Anyone I know?"

"Probably not. Let's grab some coffee soon. You can grill me then."

"It's a date. I'll call ahead and order the cheese Danish."

They said their goodbyes and Leah hung up the phone. She still had a few hours before her date with Calvin. Her fingers itched to play now that her mind has been made up. Where would she find a piano?

Grabbing her keys, Leah walked out the door and headed to the apartment below. Her hand hovered in front of the door. A wave of guilt washed over her.

Leah had befriended her neighbor just after she moved in. Their shared love for the piano cemented their friendship. When Mrs. Jacobi was diagnosed with cancer, Leah would sit and play the piano for her. But with the drama surrounding Jason and his death, Leah had not had a chance to visit the older woman.

Steeling herself, Leah knocked loudly and waited. After a few minutes, the door opened slowly. Mrs. Jacobi smiled. "Leah! How good it is to see you." She stepped aside. "Come in, come in. I just put on some water for tea."

She gave her neighbor a hug. "I am sorry I haven't been around lately. How are you doing?"

"Oh, my dear, I'm fine. I heard about your friend on the news. I wasn't upset by your absence. I knew you had your own things going on." She stepped back and eyed Leah. "You look like you could use some finger flexing."

Leah nodded, allowing the woman to lead her to the piano. She sat and played, letting the music flow through her, along with a sense of peace that she had not felt in quite awhile.

Mrs. Jacobi clapped when Leah finished her favorite piece, Rachmaninoff's *Rhapsody*. "Oh it does my heart good to hear fine music. I miss it and my students." She pointed a warning finger at Leah. "Don't forget your posture. You get so involved with the music that you forget everything else."

"Thank you, I will remember my posture."

"Good," Mrs. Jacobi said with a definitive nod. "Remember it while you play another piece for me." Her eyes took on a faraway look. "Something a bit more upbeat, perhaps?"

Pulling her shoulders back and straightening her spine, Leah threw herself into an Ellington piece that was one of her grandmother's favorites.

"Thank you, Leah." Mrs. Jacobi beamed. "Oh here I go, ordering you to entertain me! Shall I make us some tea?"

She glanced at the clock above the door. "I'm sorry, I have a date tonight."

A sparkle came into the older woman's eyes. "A date you say? Is this your first?"

"No, I think this will be our third?" She had a hard time hiding her giddy smile.

"Oh, well, then if you don't mind me giving you a little advice."

"No, ma'am, not at all." Leah sat across from her neighbor and waited for some old fashioned guidance.

"Keep your eyes wide open. People are not always as they seem."

Stars began to twinkle up in the dusky, pink sky. Leah's heart fluttered in anticipation as she followed Calvin along the dock.

They climbed onto the boat. He was a bit more gracious about it than she was. Leah hadn't developed her sea legs yet.

This is a nice boat, she thought to herself, holding tight to the seat as he guided the vessel into the water. The roar of the engine drowned out any hope of conversation.

They circled the lake for about twenty minutes before Calvin slowed down enough to cut the motor. "This is the perfect spot." He pointed to the skyline. "I love how the light hits the water. I think that would make an awesome painting."

Leah watched him spread out their meal. "You paint?"

"No," he said with a sigh. "I don't possess one artistic bone in my body."

Settling in next to him on the blanket, she looked over the food. "What is all this?"

"Well, I wasn't sure what you liked other than pasta and salad. I grabbed an assortment of deli items."

She dished some tomato and mozzarella salad onto a plate. "It all looks wonderful."

"So what about you?" He handed her a glass of wine.

"What about me?" She smiled, taking his offering.

"Are you artistic? Paint? Sculpt?"

With a nod, she answered. "I play the piano." It felt nice to say it out loud without hesitation.

"Piano? Really?" His eyes held a sparkle of something. Leah couldn't quite put her finger on it.

"Yep, I've been playing since I was a child and just decided recently to pursue my passion professionally."

"Yeah?" He took a sip of wine and snuggled in a little closer. "Is there much call for pianists around here?"

A small seed of doubt crept into her thinking. "I read an article in the paper this afternoon. There is a nationwide casting call for a Vegas production." She swallowed hard to get her words out. "I am moving in a couple of months."

His hand stopped stroking her back. "You're what?"

She swallowed a second time, wishing the news rolled off her tongue easier. "Moving to Vegas. It is a huge opportunity."

Calvin was silent for several minutes.

"Are you okay?" she asked, setting her wine aside. "You look a little pale."

"It's just," he said with a slow exhale, "I know this is only our third date, but I...there is something here...with us, and I..." His fingers ran through his blonde hair. "Okay, I am just screwing this up." Calvin turned to face Leah. "I really like you, I enjoy being with you, and I don't want to miss out on something that could have the potential to be wonderful."

Leah could feel the slow rocking of the boat underneath her. Hear the buzzing of the dragonflies skimming the water. See the light reflecting off the water. But all she could concentrate on was this man in front of her.

There was potential for a relationship. She felt an ease with Calvin that she hadn't felt in a very long time. She wished he were a bit more supportive, but maybe he was talking out of fear of losing her. What they might have. Did she want to jeopardize her future in music for what *might* happen?

"Calvin," she said, unsure of what was going to follow. "I...I really like being with you also and look forward to seeing you..."

His face broke into a smile of relief. "Really?"

"Yes, really." She returned his smile and reached for his hands. "Auditions aren't for a couple of months. In the meantime, I'll see what's available locally and we'll see where this takes us. I won't mention Vegas again unless I absolutely have to." She gave his hands a squeeze. "Deal?"

Leaning in closer, Calvin planted a soft kiss on her lips. "Deal," he said.

Chapter Eight

After tossing and turning all night with dreams of being chased by a shadow, Leah woke up with a determination to get some answers. The police didn't seem to be taking Jason's murder seriously, but someone should.

Throwing on her running shoes, the plan was simple. Go for a leisurely jog around Bright Horizons and sneak into the building to snoop around Jason's office. She continued to roll the idea around in her mind as she jogged, preparing for unforeseen circumstances. After being dismissed by Mrs. Turner, Leah wanted answers, and this was as good a plan as any to get them.

What she did not count on was Coach Turner sitting on a bench in front of the Bright Horizons Youth Group building. Slowing her gait, she debated running past him. Maybe he wouldn't notice her.

The man's eyes looked up as she approached and he smiled brightly. "Leah? Is that you?"

She nodded as her heart sank. "Hi, Mr. Turner. What are you doing out here?"

With a large shrug, the man looked forward, but didn't seem to be registering what he was seeing. "I was just thinking about life and how incredibly unexpected it is." He slid over a bit and patted the bench next to him. "Here, come, sit."

Leah grudgingly obliged. She didn't know the university coach well, but something about his demeanor indicated that he needed an ear.

"How are you feeling?"

Unconsciously rubbing the back of her head, Leah chuckled. "I'm doing fine, thank you."

"Jason was an idiot for not marrying you. I told him that too."

She blushed with embarrassment. "Well, thank you for the vote of confidence."

"He was a stubborn man, that's what made him a success," the coach began. She could see him pulling inward. "Jason was the best ball player I coached, and likable." He let out a whoosh of air. "He had a way of charming people into giving him what he wanted." Coach gave Leah a wink. "Of course, I don't need to tell you that now, do I?"

"No, sir," she agreed slowly, wondering how to tactfully extract herself from the conversation.

"Out of everyone on the team, Jason was the most successful. Knew how to play his cards right. Not that you would understand the politics of university coaching, Leah, but Jason had a gift." He gave her a sympathetic smile before continuing. "It is a big responsibility to coach, to carry the weight of a school's reputation squarely on your shoulders. Not a lot of people understand that." He patted her hand lightly. "You have to earn respect and trust. People have to love you, believe in you."

Leah sat in the silence, unsure as to whether she should say something or not. "I can see that," she finally offered.

He continued as if he hadn't heard her. "Being married to the mayor's sister does have its advantages, but my first responsibility is to my players. I found it best to ignore what everyone else told me to do and trust my gut."

"That is always a good plan." She spotted a family coming out of Bright Horizons. The boy looked familiar. With a small stomach flip, she realized it was Calvin's little boy. He looked just like his daddy.

It had never occurred to Leah to ask Calvin about his past relationships. Was this the little boy's mother? She watched the weary-looking woman referee the two children.

"Fine, I'll settle this now," the woman said with a chuckle. "No one will be watching TV until after dinner. Now Tyler, stop picking on your sister."

That got Leah's attention. Calvin had never mentioned a daughter before. Come to think of it, Calvin never really talked about his life.

"Mommy" The little girl stopped in the middle of the sidewalk. Her eyes were very serious. "Will Daddy be home for dinner tonight?"

Leah's heart clenched with sadness for the little girl. She knew she should turn away, but could not bring herself to do it. Was Calvin still married? A slow, sick churn developed in her stomach.

Sadness crossed the mother's face, but was quickly replaced by resignation. "I couldn't tell you, Sweet Pea." She cupped her daughter's chin. "We'll just wait and see, okay?"

She watched the little family climb into their car, get safely buckled in, and drive away, all while her mind was trying to conjure up every conversation she had with Calvin. Was there something she had missed? Some important piece of the puzzle to indicate he was still married? The buzzing noise in her ear began to form words and Leah realized that Coach Turner was still talking to her.

"It is time to pass the torch on to someone else," he said without realizing he had lost his audience. "To someone who will teach the fundamentals, but also inspire the love and passion for the game. Even after Jason graduated, he still held onto his passion. That is what I am looking for in my predecessor."

"Your what?" Leah finally caught up with the conversation.

"My predecessor, I'm retiring." He nodded sadly. "It's being announced at the gala."

***

Binoculars were slowly lowered, with a soft tsk. "Leah, what are you doing here?" the voice whispered. A slight frown crossed the face of the onlooker. Leah was going to be tricky. Why was she over on this side of town? She had been dismissed. There was no need for her to be here, unless...

Raising the binoculars, the observer noted the jogging shoes and running attire worn by Leah. "Ah," said the voice, "clever ruse." But thoughts swirled to the papers Leah almost found. The papers were safely tucked away, never to see the light of day.

"Just leave it be, Leah," the voice whispered. "Or else you will find yourself buried next to your precious Jason."

Chapter Nine

Pacing back and forth across the living room floor, Leah realized that she didn't have a chance of getting back into Bright Horizons and into Jason's office. The police were still dragging their feet and the killer was still out there somewhere. Leah was bound and determined to get some answers, to offer Jason some peace any way she could.

The sudden ringing of her phone caused her to jump. With her hand over her heart, she glanced at the caller ID and grimaced. Calvin. "Leave a message, buddy," she said, silencing her phone. Leah was not sure how to deal with him and was still wrestling with what she had seen that morning in the parking lot. The little girl looked unhappy and Leah's heart went out to the mother who looked vacant. If she'd known Calvin was married, she would have never agreed to go out with him in the first place. That is *if* Calvin was married.

"Not now!" she told herself, shifting her thought process back to the task of solving Jason's murder. Then it dawned on her to go to Jason's house. The clock read three-fifteen. Little Jay-Jay got picked up from day care at three-thirty. He and Rosa wouldn't get home until four if traffic was decent. With a small frown, Leah found it sad that she knew their schedule so well. "Water under the bridge," she said, grabbing her car keys. Keys? How was she going to get into the house without one?

Turning the ignition over in her car, she backed out of her parking space. Tanvir. Tanvir had a key. He and Jason had been house mates before Rosa got pregnant and moved in. But Leah had not seen nor heard from Tanvir since the day of her attack which seemed odd, but then again, she had been banned from Bright Horizons. Maybe it wasn't so odd.

Leah remembered the spare key hidden under the bird feeder on the side of the house. With a sigh of relief, she urged her car forward with a small boost in confidence. Her mother's voice softly nagged in the back of her mind. It droned on about sin, coveting thy neighbor's possessions, and breaking the law in general. Leah reasoned that she was doing a good thing by helping the police. She drove past Jason's house twice to make sure there was no sign of movement in the windows and Rosa's car was not anywhere to be seen.

Taking a deep breath, she parked a block down and over just to be on the safe side.

The house sat in an affluent neighborhood. Tongues wagged quite a bit when Jason purchased his house so quickly out of college. There was a lot of speculation over the Turners helping him out financially, but the rumors died down once Bright Horizons became a steady beacon of hope for troubled youth.

Quickly making her way to the house and the bird feeder, Leah boosted the key and walked confidently to the front door. With shaky fingers, she worked the lock until there was an audible click of the tumblers.

"Okay," she whispered, turning the knob. Pausing at the open door, she listened for any sign of movement. "So far so good." Stepping into the airy living room brought back memories, both good and bad.

Leah wondered how Rosa continued to live here after what had happened. She wasn't sure she could. If Rosa didn't have such an airtight alibi, Leah would have pegged her for the murder. *She certainly is scary enough*, Leah thought nervously as she made her way to Jason's office. But attending her mother's 60th birthday celebration 45 miles away with 100 other guests gave Rosa a credible accounting for her whereabouts.

Once inside the study, Leah began rifling through papers, scanning everything she got her hands on, looking for some glaring piece of evidence. She came across a packet of legal documents and her heart skipped a beat. It was paperwork for Jason seeking sole custody of little Jay-Jay. Was he planning on breaking up with Rosa and taking their son? Leah couldn't imagine Rosa sitting by and doing nothing to stop it. Killing Jason? Maybe, but according to the newspaper, everyone at the party vouched for her.

Folding the papers up and putting them back into the drawer, she turned to another section of the office when the front door opened. Her heart stopped beating. The small *thump, thump, thump* of little feet barreled through the living room.

"Take your shoes off, Jay-Jay, and come in the kitchen for a snack," Rosa's voice drifted through the house.

Leah stood frozen behind the desk as the thumping grew louder and headed right toward her. Trapped, Leah quickly crouched behind the desk, and accidentally knocked over a pencil holder. She silently cursed herself while holding her breath scared to make another sound. The boy skidded to a stop in front of the open door and gave the room a quizzical look. Then without another thought, he took off down the hall to his bedroom.

Breathing a sigh of relief, Leah was glad to hear little Jay-Jays footsteps echo down the hall. She needed to get out of the house. Fast.

A steady whack of metal hitting a cutting board caused Leah to break out into a cold sweat. Leah tiptoed down the hall. She had no idea what Rosa was cutting in the kitchen, but it sounded as if the action was done with accuracy and a lot of determination.

WHACK

"Do you want peanut butter or cream cheese on your celery sticks?" Rosa asked little Jay-Jay.

WHACK

Leah inched along the wall quietly. She was sure her loud heartbeat would give her away. With a sweat-drenched, shaky hand, Leah cracked open the back door.

WHACK

She slipped out into the backyard, sprinted through the gate, and down the street. The persistent whack of Rosa's chopping rang in Leah's head for the rest of the night.

Chapter Ten

The café was virtually empty when Leah arrived. Checking her watch, she realized she was running early. Winding her way through the maze of tables, she settled into a corner booth and waited.

Quincy followed her by five minutes. After exchanging a round of hugs, he sat opposite of her. "It is really good to see you." He smiled. "Thank you for arranging this. The way my schedule is shaping up, I won't get a hot meal outside of my office for another two years."

Her head bobbed with sympathy. "The gala." Leah could not stop the sigh that escaped. "It was a mess when Mrs. Turner called me in. How is it shaping up?"

Taking a menu, Quincy shrugged. "I couldn't tell you. She has split the to-do list and delegated half the staff to do their own little part."

"Oh that sounds like a disaster waiting to happen." Leah shuddered, scanning the menu.

He said without looking up, "It can't be any worse than the food poisoning gala."

She grasped her stomach with a laugh. "Oh I had almost forgotten that one! Thanks for reminding me." The menu was quickly forgotten. "How about the one with the streaking protester?"

"Oh yes! I had forgotten about the incredibly endowed gentleman who wanted to bring notice to our declining sea life."

"Until he realized he was at the wrong fundraiser." She continued laughing harder. "I still gave to his charity only to erase the image from my mind."

"I bet you are the only one from the gala who did."

Leah pushed at the menu. "Yeah, well, everyone has different priorities." The conversation was momentarily delayed by the server.

"So" Quincy leaned in after their order had been taken. "You ready to tell me about this date you had the other night?"

Flashes of water, sunset, and a sad little girl rushed through Leah's head. "His name is Calvin. We had an amazing evening. I really like him, but..." She waited a beat before telling Quincy what she had witnessed outside of Bright Horizons.

He shook his head. "Calvin is bad news. Lots of emotional baggage comes with him."

He took her hand gently. "Concentrate on your self for once. You don't need a man to complete you."

"I just feel so alone."

"What you need is to pursue your dream," Quincy insisted. "You're young, you're smart, and you are unattached. Explore the country. Play piano for tips to get you to the next town. Settle in Vegas. Whatever you decide to do, do it for yourself. Not for Calvin, and definitely not for Jason."

Her head snapped at the mention of Jason's name. "Did Jason ever tell you that he was seeking sole custody of little Jay-Jay?"

Emotions flickered across his face too fast for Leah to recognize. Quincy's expression settled into a passive stance. "Wouldn't surprise me. There was a lot of negativity going on in that house. The cops had been called a couple of times due to Rosa's fiery personality." His eyes narrowed. "How did you find this out?"

Leah squirmed a little in the booth. "I sort of broke into his house and ransacked his study."

Quincy's eyes almost bulged out of his head. "Are you nuts? Why would you do something like that?"

"Cops are dragging their feet, Quincy. They don't care who murdered Jason, and I felt compelled to get to the bottom of it, or at the very least to offer them a lead."

Several minutes passed before Quincy spoke. "All we can do is speculate; let the police do their job, Leah. Jason is the only one with answers, and no amount of snooping in the world is going to bring him back to tell us what they are."

Later that evening, Leah found herself at Mrs. Jacobi's

delivering a tray piled with chicken soup, crackers, tea, and cookies.

"Oh, such a dear," the older woman said as she opened the door. "And dinner too? You are too good to me. How are you doing?"

"Just fine, Mrs. Jacobi." Leah set the tray down on a TV stand and wheeled it over to her neighbor. "Come and sit before the soup cools."

"Tell me, how did your date go?" The woman's eyes sparkled with delight.

Leah nodded slowly. "Fine. It went fine." Her eyes glanced over to the piano and she turned back to Mrs. Jacobi.

"Play something for me while I eat, please."

"Sure." Leah repressed her sigh of relief. Although she thoroughly enjoyed her neighbor's company, Leah was itching to play. "Do you have any requests?"

"Brahms *Sonata Number One in C major*. Are you familiar?"

"I believe I am." Leah turned to the keys and lightly touched them, picturing the keystrokes in her mind before she began.

Mrs. Jacobi took a sip of soup. "Don't forget your posture. The melody should lift the weight of the world from your shoulders."

Her fingers flew across the ivories; Leah allowed her mind to wander as the music filled her...

The night sky was filled with twinkling stars. Leah and Jason spread a blanket on the grass and enjoyed the peace of his backyard. They stared up at the velvet sky in amicable silence.

"If you could make one wish, what would it be?" Leah asked quietly.

He was silent for a long time, staring up at the stars. Leah wasn't sure if he had heard her. "Ever since I was a kid, I wished trees had talked," he finally answered.

Leah could not help but roll her eyes. "You are such a freak, Jason."

He fed her a cherry from the bowl between them. "Imagine it, Leah; trees are the oldest things on the earth. Some of them have been around for hundreds of years. Can you imagine the stories they would tell?"

Leah thought about it a moment. "If your wish came true and ten years from now this tree was to tell our story, what would it say?"

His eyes went back to the stars. He finally reached over, squeezed her hand, and pulled her in for a long, slow kiss. There was never a shortage of him showing his love for her. She just wanted to hear him say the words...

Leah's fingers hit the last note and let it reverberate in the air. Feeling the vibration of the lingering melody filled her with confidence. With a triumphant smile, she turned back to Mrs. Jacobi, who had fallen asleep in her recliner.

Grabbing a throw from the couch, Leah covered the older woman, put the food in the fridge, and made sure the door was locked behind her. Taking the stairs two at a time, she thought this feeling of elation could carry her through any-thing. Nothing could bring her down, except maybe the handsome blonde sitting at her door waiting for her.

Calvin stood up when he saw her. "Hello, Leah."

Chapter Eleven

The distance between herself and Calvin was twenty steps. Leah's tension grew with each footfall. "What are you doing here, Calvin?"

He pulled a small bouquet of flowers out from behind his back. "Well, I hadn't heard from you and was concerned."

Casting a glance at the flowers, she left them to wilt in his hand. "Well, as you can see, I'm fine."

A look of confusion passed over his face. "Are you avoiding me for some reason?"

Leah suddenly felt incredibly uncomfortable. Her feelings were still up in the air about what she had seen and she wasn't entirely happy that he was pushing the issue before she was ready to talk. "Look, Calvin, I am incredibly busy and..." She reached for the doorknob, but he stepped in her way.

"Leah, what is it? I thought we had a great time watching the sunset. I told you how I felt about you."

"But you left out the part that you were married." Her breath caught. Leah was hoping, praying that she was reading way too much into the situation. *Please let me be wrong,* she pleaded silently. The panicked look on his face confirmed her fears.

"I...but...don't..." he stammered. "Why?" He cleared his throat. "Why would you think that?"

"I saw your wife outside of Bright Horizons with your son Tyler and a little girl." Her arms folded protectively across her chest, her anger cranked up a notch. "The little girl was asking if you were going to be home for dinner." The dumbfounded look on his face made her even angrier.

"Leah, I..." He passed a hand over his smooth-shaven

face. "It's a complicated situation."

"Let me make it simple for you. I do *not* date married men!"

"We are separated," he said quickly. "A divorce is just around the corner."

She shook her head; her arms tightened across her chest. "I cannot believe you put me in this position."

Calvin took a step closer. "My marriage has been dead for years. I only stayed for my children."

"Just leave me alone, Calvin. I have never been in this situation before and really don't need this uncertainty in my life right now."

He took another small step forward and reached for her. His hand lightly rested on her shoulder. "Please don't push me away, Leah." His second hand fell on the opposite shoulder.

With arms still folded across her chest, she was pulled into his strong embrace.

"Please, Leah," he pleaded. "You just need to trust me."

Tanvir glanced at the clock on his desk and was surprised to see how late it was. The whir of the janitor's vacuum down the hall made his head pound in double time.

Bright Horizons had become a three-ring circus, he thought, popping two Motrin into his mouth. Maybe he could squeeze in a drink on his way home. He certainly needed it. It seemed as if he had lost control over this organization.

More like Mrs. Turner had lost control since she was running the place now. She had no idea how much Bright Horizons was indebted to him. He had been here since day one and practically built this business with his two hands.

Jason was the one with the face and the charm. *Everyone* loved Jason. No one cared about the person behind him doing all the tedious grunt work, making sure that the organization was a success.

It was obvious people were only nice to him because he was Jason's best friend, his right-hand man. Tanvir grimaced. He didn't care that he was outshined by the memory of his dead friend. Tanvir had bigger plans and had no intention of being Jason's puppet forever. He had his aim set much higher, taking over the head coach position at the university.

For years, Tanvir had been studying play books and the strategies of other teams. Coach Turner took him under his wing and allowed him on the sidelines of games to "embrace the action." But he knew deep down that Jason, the golden boy, would be the one tapped to replace Coach Turner, no matter how much legwork Tanvir put in. Not because Jason knew the game better, but because he was good at keeping secrets. There was a price, however, for keeping a secret for too long.

Maybe, just maybe, Tanvir finally had the upper hand.

Chapter Twelve

The steady *squeak, squeak* of the swing grated on Rosa's frayed nerves. Little Jay-Jay's laughter was the only thing keeping her from snapping. Bringing him to the park was a much better alternative than shopping with Mrs. Turner at Neiman Marcus. The older woman seemed to think she needed a new gown for the gala.

Rosa didn't care about the gala, didn't care about Bright Horizons, and certainly didn't care for Mrs. Turner. Now that Jason was dead, what did she need to suck up to them for? She got a healthy settlement to care for little Jay-Jay. *Would have been bigger if he had married me,* Rosa thought bitterly. But she really couldn't complain much. She was financially comfortable, lived in a nice home with a closet full of designer clothes, and drove a nice car.

Not that piece of crap Taurus I was driving when I met Jason. Rosa shuddered remembering the pile of bills in her cramped efficiency apartment with no air conditioning. Working twelve hour shifts trying to make ends meet.

Since she met Jason, she had sucked up to Mrs. Turner, knowing the woman signed the checks. Rosa turned a blind eye to the heavy flirtation between the two that kept the waters calm and the money rolling in. There was no way she was going back to working her fingers to the bone and having nothing to show for it.

Rosa's anger simmered remembering the conversation she overheard the day before at Bright Horizons. Quincy was telling Mrs. Turner about Leah and how she was thinking about moving to Las Vegas to play the piano or something equally as senseless. Rosa's first thought was good riddance;

at least she wouldn't have to worry about running into her around town.

She had also learned while eavesdropping that Leah had taken up with a married man. It didn't surprise her. Rosa knew all about Leah's flings when her relationship with Jason was "off." She always came back to Jason in tears, saying how sorry she was. Then Jason would forgive her. What a waste of space she was.

Before Rosa could walk away from her eavesdropping, she overheard Quincy mention that Leah had broken into her house. Rosa stood rooted to the spot. *That foolish woman broke into my house*? *MY HOUSE!* She remembered looking into Jason's study and it being messier than usual, but only assumed it was the overly curious toddler running amok. Rosa could feel the heat of anger engulf her as she quietly walked out of the Bright Horizons building, deciding to come back when no one else was around.

"Mommy!" Little Jay-Jay tugged at her skirt and brought her back to the present. "Slide, wanna go slide?"

Taking his hand, she led him over to the slide. In the back of her mind, she couldn't help but wonder if Leah had taken anything from her home. Her first instinct was to confront Leah and put her in her place. But Rosa settled on a better plan.

A cool breeze broke the heat of the sun on Leah's back. She was not sure how it happened, but she found herself fishing with Calvin on his boat.

"Now if you take the worm." He pulled out a long, plump one out of the bowl of dirt. "Then slide it onto the..."

She turned her head away with an audible, "*Ugh*!"

"Not a fan yet, huh?"

Shaking her head, she turned enough to look with one eye, keeping the other firmly closed. "My father used to fish when I was a little girl. He used fresh shrimp, less wiggly."

Calvin handed her the pole. "Cast it lightly." Putting his arms around her, he showed her the proper casting technique.

A fish bit almost instantly. With a bit of fumbling and a lot of laughing, they finally got the baby blue gill reeled in. "I have never caught a fish before!" Leah exclaimed.

"Grab the fish like this." Calvin positioned her one hand and guided her other to remove the hook.

Leah did so reluctantly. The fish was more slimy and squirmy than the worm looked. She quickly tossed the fish back into the lake. "Blech!" She moved the pole and hooked her finger.

"Aw." Calvin winced. "It doesn't look too bad. I have a band-aid here in the first-aid kit." He gently taped her cut and kissed it slowly. "You have beautiful fingers, very long."

She reclaimed her hand. "That's what my grandmother told me." She wiggled her fingers in the air. "Natural piano fingers."

"Care to try it again?" he asked, picking up the pole.

"Uh no, thanks." She opened a bottle of water. "I'd rather just talk, if you don't mind."

"Okay." He cast his line into the water. "What do you want to talk about?"

"Your marriage."

He did a double take. "You don't waste any time, do you?"

"No sir, I told you I don't date married men and you said to trust you." She wiped her hands with a wet napkin. "You want my trust? I need answers."

With a slow nod, Calvin agreed to answer any questions she had.

"What happened between you two?"

"How much time have you got?" He chuckled. "We have nothing in common. I like to go out and do things. Marla is more of a homebody, preferring to watch a DVD than go to the theater.

"Her name is Marla?"

He nodded. "Yes, her name is Marla. I thought I was in love when we got married, but it quickly became evident that we weren't in love. Then she became pregnant with Tyler and we decided to make a go of it, see what happened. By the time Amanda was born..."

"Amanda is your daughter?"

"Yeah" His smile was that of a proud father. "She is my princess. I love my kids; they are great." Calvin looked at Leah for a long moment. "Maybe you could meet them sometime."

Leah shifted uncomfortably under Calvin's gaze.

Grabbing her hand, he gave a gentle squeeze. "It has been a long time since I have felt this happy. You have to know that."

"I will keep that in mind." Offering a small smile, she patted his hand. "Let's just enjoy the beauty of the day."

Arm in arm, Leah and Calvin headed up the steps to her apartment. They chatted quietly about the evening ahead of them. An envelope was taped to her door. "This must be my lease renewal papers." She took the envelope off her door. "I need to turn in my notice."

"You know, I am sleeping on a buddy's couch right now. If you are apartment hunting, maybe we can..."

Leah chose to ignore the obvious hint Calvin just dropped. She slipped a finger under the flap of the envelope, pulled out a single sheet of paper, and read the gothic print: *Pretty Girls Can Die Too*

Leah stood rooted in panic. She could feel the pulse in her neck beating violently. Her mother's voice broke through her fear, reminding her that the wages of sin is death.

Chapter Thirteen

The threat of the letter rattled Leah to the core. She was grateful Calvin had insisted on staying with her last night to keep her company. He kept her somewhat distracted with movies and useless trivia, but the gothic letters ran like a ticker tape through her mind. Calvin served her breakfast in bed before heading off to work. Once she heard the door click behind him, she realized she was all alone and vulnerable.

"Enough, Leah!" she said out loud. "Get a grip!" Leah made up her mind to call Detective Becky. It might not hurt talking to a professional, she reasoned.

The detective's business card turned over in Leah's fingertips. She picked up the phone a couple times and replaced it quickly. Maybe she was being too rash, she thought. Instead of calling the police department, Leah dialed Quincy instead.

"Yah?" He answered on the third ring.

"Hey, Quincy, it's Leah."

"Now's not a good time." His tone was rushed and a bit gruff.

"Oh, I'm sorry. I just need to..."

"I'm with Mrs. Turner. I'll call you later."

Before she could get in another word, the line went dead. *Must be doing last minute gala stuff*, she thought with a small smile. *I don't envy them*. Leah headed into her living room and started to pack.

Time for me to move on, wherever the wind may take me.

A few hours later, Leah's stomach gave off a low, angry rumble. Glancing at the clock, she was shocked to see how late it was. Quickly whipping up a couple tuna sandwiches and heating up some soup, Leah headed downstairs to check on her neighbor.

After the initial knock, Leah waited a minute or two before knocking again. She waited a few more minutes and felt a little apprehension. As her mouth opened to call out to Mrs. Jacobi, the door opened slowly.

The older woman looked frail and exhausted. "Sorry, Leah." Her voice was a raspy whisper. "I didn't mean to keep you waiting. How are you, dear?"

"I'm fine, Mrs. Jacobi." She tried to keep her voice light, but the sight of her friend cracked her heart. Placing the tray down on the coffee table, Leah laid out some food on the TV stand. "I brought you some lunch."

Mrs. Jacobi waved a hankie. "No, Leah." She covered her mouth to cough. "I really don't seem to have much of an appetite today, but I would love for you to play something. It gives me such great comfort to hear your music."

"Do you have any requests?" Leah tripped over herself to get to the piano, her fingers itching to pound out anything to put a smile on her neighbor's face.

The older woman was lost in thought for a moment. "Do you know the song *Unforgettable*?"

Leah turned to the keys and thought for a moment, trying to conjure the song. "I do believe I know the song," she said, tapping the keys, trying to find the right combination of notes. "Fell in love with it when Nat King Cole's daughter re-released it several years ago." The melody came back to her and she began to play the requested song. "Is this the song?" The dreamy smile on Mrs. Jacobi's face was her answer. When the song was over, Leah turned back to face the older woman. "You look like the cat that ate the canary," she teased. "Was that a song you shared with Mr. Jacobi?"

"No." The dreamy faraway look was still in her eye. "No, that was the song I shared with my first love, Ben."

Leah slipped off the piano bench and knelt in front of Mrs. Jacobi. "What happened between you and Ben?"

"It seems like just yesterday when I was young and rebellious, trying to find myself. I didn't know what I wanted." She gave a soft chuckle. "Ben and I were just mad for each other, but the timing was all off." The older woman took a picture off a table. "I became pregnant with my sweet Rosie."

Leah looked at the plump face, mass of bright curls, and serious eyes. "She is adorable."

Mrs. Jacobi nodded, "She was an adorable baby and grew into a striking young woman. She was the apple of my eye."

Placing the photo back onto the table, she continued. "Of course back in the sixties, having a baby out of wedlock was so taboo. My family disowned me. So Ben and I packed up my Thunderbird and tried to make a go of it, but with the baby came responsibility, and it wasn't in the cards for us." Sadness passed across her face. "He enlisted in the army, was sent over to Vietnam, and never came home."

"Oh, I am so sorry to hear that." Leah touched the older woman's hand.

Mrs. Jacobi patted her hand. "Life has a funny way of working out. I went to school, became a music teacher, and met a gifted composer, Mr. Francis Jacobi."

She pulled another frame from the table. The faded photo inside showed a much younger Mrs. Jacobi, a tall, sturdy man, and the little girl with serious eyes and blonde curls. They stood in front of a little white chapel.

"Oh there was such a fuss when Frank and I were married. We had only known each other for a few months, but were together for fifty years before he passed."

She leaned back in the recliner, her precious energy spent on storytelling, "We never had children of our own, but he treated my little Rosie like she was his."

"What made Frank so special?" Leah asked, captivated by Mrs. Jacobi's story.

The dreamlike smile played about her lips, "He loved me unconditionally. Accepted everything about me, flaws and all." Her eyes drooped. "Didn't ask me to be someone I wasn't and didn't try to change me. Loved me and my Rosie. We were one small, happy family."

Leah let go of the woman's hand, took the throw off the couch, and covered Mrs. Jacobi.

The older woman's eyes opened again. "Don't you fret, dear. Your Prince Charming is out there waiting for you." She reached up and patted Leah's cheek. "You need to find yourself first, before he finds you."

Tucking the throw around her frail body, Leah bid her good night. "I'll come by tomorrow to play some more music."

"I would love to hear *The Way We Were*," Mrs. Jacobi

murmured before drifting back off to sleep.

Tossing and turning all night, Leah drifted in and out of sleep. Every small noise caused her to sit up and wonder if someone was breaking in. She gave up trying to sleep around five a.m. and continued packing.

A sudden knock on the door startled Leah. She dribbled coffee down her shirt front. "And a good morning to me," she muttered, dabbing at her chest and heading to the door.

The knock erupted again. She looked through the peephole. The distorted face of a vaguely familiar woman stood on the other side. Leah hesitated a moment longer before opening the door a crack. The blonde woman stood with a shaky confidence...it was the eyes, those bright, serious eyes that she had seen the night before.

"Hello. Are you Leah?" the woman asked.

"Yes," Leah replied nervously. Her heartbeat doubled. "Are you Rosie?" Leah's mouth went dry. The question came out in a hoarse whisper.

The woman cleared her throat. "Yes, my name is Roseanne. My mother was your neighbor downstairs."

The unease grew before Leah stepped aside to invite Roseanne in. "Could I offer you something to drink? I have a fresh pot of coffee."

Roseanne shook her head; a curl escaped from the pile on her head. "No, no thank you. I can't stay." She smoothed down the front of her blazer. "I just came by to inform you that my mother passed away last night."

Leah sank into the nearest chair. "What? No. I just saw her yesterday. We had lunch together. She asked me to come by tonight to play for her." Tears welled up in her eyes. "*The Way We Were.*"

A small twitch of a smile pulled at Roseanne's mouth. "That was my father's favorite song." The casual tone switched back into business as she continued. "My mother spoke very highly of you. Thank you for keeping her company." She squared her shoulders. "I may not have been the best daughter in the world, but I loved my mother very much." Her voice caught slightly. "She encouraged me to follow my dreams and to live life to the fullest." A tear escaped and rolled down her full cheek.

Handing her a Kleenex, Leah led the woman to the couch.

Roseanne dabbed at her eyes. "As an anthropologist, I travel a lot and I am really thankful you were here to comfort her."

Leah took hold of Roseanne's hands. "Your mother spoke very highly of you too," she said softly. "Yesterday she told me how much joy you brought her. She loved you very much."

The well of tears finally overflowed. Leah wrapped the blonde woman up in her arms and held her close as they both mourned the woman who encouraged them to follow their dreams.

Sitting up, Rosanne dabbed at her eyes again with a fresh Kleenex. "The movers are coming in to pack up mother's belongings. But she left something for you."

"Me?" Leah asked, blotting her tears away. "What could she possibly leave me? She had given me so much already."

Roseanne walked to the door and opened it. Down the hall, two moving men were clearing the final step and heading toward her apartment. "She wanted you to have her piano." Roseanne smiled. "And this." Leah saw her name scrawled in big looping letters across an envelope. The raised black musical notes swam in her vision as tears threatened to pour.

"Take care, Leah," Roseanne said as she walked out the door.

That night, Leah poured herself a goblet of red wine and sat at the piano bench. Her fingers trailed over the keys before finally setting her glass down and playing Mrs. Jacobi's final request. She was not Streisand, but Leah felt compelled to sing the haunting lyrics as she played *The Way We Were*.

When Leah finished singing the last note, she raised her glass. "Good night, Mrs. Jacobi," she whispered before taking a long sip. Her eyes fell on the envelope sitting on top of the piano. Fingering the raised notes, Leah took another sip before opening the letter. It was a single handwritten page on matching stationery.

My Dear Leah,
Never let the weight of the world hold you down. Remember your dreams are at your fingertips. Reach out and let the music set you free.
Mrs. Jacobi

Chapter Fourteen

Papers and playbooks littered Tanvir's desk. He had been tirelessly reworking old plays to give them new twists and make them fresh. *Defense needs to tighten up if we have any hopes to make it to playoffs,* he thought. *I really should be running this with the team.*

Footsteps in the hall froze Tanvir to his seat. Mrs. Turner was supposed to be getting her hair done. She shouldn't be back this soon. The woman would not hesitate tearing into him if he was found working on anything other than gala preparations. Tanvir had no desire to be on the receiving end of a Turner tongue lashing and did a slow exhale when the footfalls grew fainter.

Gathering his courage and plays, Tanvir headed out to talk with Coach Turner before practice. This is the last game before the gala, the last game before Coach announced his retirement.

Coach Turner waved Tanvir into his office before the younger man could knock. The coach was on the phone, his full face a bit on the flushed side. "No, she's out getting her hair done." He motioned for Tanvir to sit.

"I don't know why she's not answering her phone, she's your sister. Maybe her nails are too wet to press a button." His laugh sounded a bit brittle.

"No, I can't, I have practice soon. If I see her, I'll have her call you." He nodded. "Yep, all right, see ya."

Tanvir watched the coach hang up the phone with a heavy sigh. "A bit of advice, don't marry into a political family." He grabbed the sport coat draped across the back of the office chair. "I'm sure you can imagine the headaches."

"Yes sir," Tanvir agreed with a nervous laugh. "Um, I have been reworking some defensive moves and think..."

Coach took the papers and scanned them. "Oh yeah, I see." He nodded with appreciation before laying them on the desk. "Very impressive, Tanvir." He grabbed his whistle off the back of the door and put it in his coat pocket. "Now if you'll excuse me, I have practice." Placing his hat squarely on his head, he patted Tanvir's shoulder. "Mrs. Turner is swamped with gala preparations. I hope you appreciate what an asset you are in this organization. This will be the largest gala Bright Horizons has ever hosted."

Tanvir stood speechless, unsure of what to say.

Coach took a final look around and patted himself down, making sure he had everything. "I sure hope Quincy has started the warm up drills. If not, that just puts me further behind."

"Excuse me, sir." Tanvir's voice croaked in disbelief. "Quincy?"

With a nod, the older man said, "Yeah, Quincy is helping with the coaching staff." He picked up Tanvir's plays and shoved them into his breast pocket. "Thanks for the defense strategies. We are going to need all the help we can get!" With a final slap to Tanvir's arm, Coach Turner strode down the hallway.

Tanvir stood in the doorway shaking with rage. He could not believe that his loyalty to this organization had been slighted once again. That Coach Turner had turned his back on him so quickly and that Quincy was now the newest threat to his future.

Calvin turned into the familiar driveway of Marla's townhouse. He sat in his SUV for a moment eyeing the windows. Handlebars from a new bike poked up from the back. He couldn't help but smile.

Marla had called to tell him Tyler had a really good report card. As promised, Calvin replaced the bike he had run over. He also bought Amanda a tea set. As long as Marla said they were good, Calvin bought presents for them. The kids didn't seem to be taking the separation well.

Amanda's squeals of delight broke into his thoughts.

"Daddy's here, daddy's here."

As soon as his feet hit the driveway, a forty-five pound whirlwind of activity knocked him against the vehicle.

"Hi, Daddy!" She giggled, climbing up his legs.

He lifted her up. "Hi, princess."

"Mommy said I could have popcorn. Can I have popcorn, please, please, please?"

Calvin carried her into the house. "If Mommy said you could have popcorn, then yes, I will get you some popcorn."

"Yay! Mommy! I can have popcorn!" Amanda crawled down out of her father's grasp and began to skip in circles chanting, "I can have some popcorn; I can have some popcorn!"

Tyler sulked into the living room. "Hey, champ!" Calvin pulled his son into a hug, "Mom tells me you brought home a good report card."

The boy nodded, keeping his eyes on the floor.

"Well, a promise is a promise." Calvin nudged his son's shoulder. "Get your shoes on. Someone left something for you in my car."

Tyler's face lightened a little. "Really?" he asked with a half-smile.

Amanda stopped skipping and slammed into Calvin's legs. "Did someone leave something for me too?"

"I do believe they did. Get your shoes on. Both of you!"

The kids ran up the stairs, almost knocking their mother over in their haste.

Marla came into the room with a cleaning rag in her hands. "What time will you be back from the movies tonight?"

"Shouldn't be too late. I was going to take them out for ice cream afterwards."

She nodded slowly. "Okay, I'll just keep the door unlocked for you then."

"Okay," he said quietly. It was an irritating gesture when Marla had the locks changed, but he knew it was her way of dealing with the separation.

The kids barreled back into the room. "Come on, Mom." Tyler grabbed her hand, pulling her to the door. "Come see what I got."

Amanda, close on her brother's heels, grabbed her mother's other hand and pulled. "Yeah, come see, come see!"

Reluctantly, Marla allowed herself to be pulled outside by her children.

Calvin first pulled out Tyler's bike. "Here you go, champ!" he said, putting it down on the ground. "Just make sure you take care of it and put it in the garage when you're done riding it."

"I will, Dad." Tyler climbed up onto the seat and checked out the brakes and gears.

Calvin tousled his son's head before turning to the jumping whirlwind next to him.

"What's in there for me? What's in there for me?" she asked with excitement, clapping her hands.

Calvin went to the back seat and pulled out his daughter's present. "Every princess needs her own tea set."

Amanda's eyes went wide. "Oh, Daddy, thank you!" She turned to Marla. "Mommy? Can I have tea with my popcorn at the movies?"

Marla cupped her daughter's cheek. "I'm afraid not, sweet pea. How about if I take it inside and you can have a formal tea party tomorrow?"

The little girl seemed to mull the compromise over in her mind.

"I will even let you wear my special beads and heels."

"Okay." Her face brightened as she handed her mother the box. "Come on, Daddy, I want my popcorn!" She climbed into the back seat.

Tyler put his bike safely in the garage and slowly walked back to the car. "Do you want to come with us, Mommy?" he asked quietly.

"Oh, Ty, I wish I could, but I've got a lot of work to do here," she said as she gave him a kiss. "You have fun with Daddy. Enjoy the movie!"

The boy nodded, his eyes downcast, and climbed slowly into the back seat.

Calvin made sure they were safely buckled in before closing the door. "I'm okay with you coming to the movies with us. It might be more fun than adding numbers."

"Cal, don't." She sighed. "I don't want to confuse the kids."

He cast a look at the sad face of his son. The little boy's eyes were wary as he watched the verbal exchange. "I don't see what the confusion is. They are having a hard time with the separation. Maybe if we all spent time together..."

"Stop it, Calvin," Marla's voice held a tone of controlled anger he had become all too familiar with lately. "Just stop."

"Look, I don't want to spend the entire car ride explaining

to them why you didn't come." He allowed his anger to get the better of him.

"Don't make a scene in front of the kids." She folded her arms tightly across her chest.

"You know you're beautiful when you get all sanctimonious and huffy." He smiled, taking a step closer.

She rolled her eyes, but a small smile started to emerge. "Don't you try to sweet talk me. I know all your tricks."

"No tricks. Come on out with us. Watch a movie, have some ice cream..."

"And popcorn!" Amanda yelled from the back seat.

Calvin and Marla looked and saw Tyler had the door open and both children were watching them intently.

Marla rolled her eyes again. "Fine." She laughed.

"Hooray!" the children yelled.

"Give me two minutes to change." She glared playfully at Calvin, "You will pay for this."

"Oh, I am scared," he retorted, heading to the car. "Do you see me shaking?"

After the movie, they all settled into a booth at the ice cream shop. Amanda and Tyler ate their cones and chatted about the movie. Marla picked at the sundae she and Calvin were sharing.

He could not help but notice how beautiful Marla looked tonight. What happened to their marriage? Why had it unraveled so badly? His daughter's excited voice broke into his thought process.

"It was the *swoosh, swoosh.*" Amanda demonstrated with her ice cream cone the sweeping arc of a flying broomstick. "And the *whoa!*" Her cone went up and down.

"Amanda," Marla warned with a smile, "you're going to lose your ice cream if you aren't careful."

"Sorry, Mommy." She brought the cone back to her mouth. "I love pink ice cream."

"I know you do, sweet pea." Marla smiled, handing her daughter a napkin. "How you doing, little man? Did you enjoy the movie?"

Tyler nodded, eating his ice cream. "It was fun. The book had more stuff in it, though, but I liked the final battle scene when he pulled the sword out of the hat, that was cool."

Calvin marveled at her ease with the children. It just made her radiate.

"What are you looking at?" she asked, dabbing at her mouth.

He said, clearing his throat, "You're probably going to steal the cherry."

"You know it," she laughed, popping the red orb into her mouth.

"Can I have a cherry?" Amanda asked, a pout starting to form.

"Sorry, sweetie, cherries don't come with ice cream cones."

The pout became more prominent. "I want a cherry."

Calvin gathered her into his arms. "How about if I bring you your own cherries next time I come visit?"

She nodded, wiping away her tears. "Okay, Daddy."

He held her close. Amanda had a long day and she was suffering from the irrationality of an exhausted five-year-old. "Why don't we finish up here and get going?"

When they arrived home, Calvin carried his sleeping daughter up to her room and tucked her in. Stopping by his son's room, he gave hugs, kisses, and promises of longer visits.

Marla was found in the kitchen pouring hot water into a teapot. "I thought the tea party was tomorrow?" he joked.

With a blank expression, she pulled a large envelope out from her purse and placed it on the counter in front of him.

His hands shook as he picked it up.

"Papers are in order, please review and sign them."

Calvin felt as if he had been sucker punched. "What? But Marla, I thought."

"Please, Calvin; I have had a long day. Would you please just go? You can bring the papers over next time you visit." Her tone was forced and unnatural.

"I thought we were just taking a break." He felt like his family was ebbing away out of his grasp. "I'm not ready for a divorce."

She shook her head. "I can't do this anymore, Calvin. I don't want to live my life waiting for you to decide whether or not we are a priority."

Tears welled up in his eyes as he pulled Marla into a tight embrace. He held her close, smelling her strawberry shampoo. Calvin loved the smell of strawberries. He whispered into her hair, "Marla, please, please! I am not ready to let go. You have to learn to trust me again."

The sudden rapping on the front door caused Leah to jump out of her skin. She wondered briefly if it was the psycho taping another letter to her door. Looking out the peep hole, Leah exhaled heavily.

"Hey, Quincy!" She held the door open for him, gesturing with a free hand. "Come in."

He kissed her cheek as he passed. "Hey yourself." Eyeing the piles of boxes, he asked, "What's going on?"

"This is my cathartic way of gaining perspective." Her laugh trailed behind her as she headed into the kitchen.

Quincy followed. "I really am sorry about the other day."

"The other day?" Leah shook her head in confusion. "What other day?"

"When I blew you off? It was not my intention."

She took a moment to think. "On the phone!" With a wave of her hand, she continued. "Please don't worry about it. I *know* how stressful planning a huge charity event can be. The upcoming gala is the largest one ever for Bright Horizons and I can imagine how frazzled everyone is."

Nodding his head, he took a piece of cheese from the dish on the counter. "I am not an event planner by any means, but I am expected to pitch in and help. The entire staff is required to help with this lavish affair. On top of that, I have been helping out with coaching duties."

Leah handed him a glass of wine. Taking the cheese dish, they wandered into the living room. "So you are pulling double duty?"

"Uh, yeah." He took a sip of the dry red wine and sucked in his cheeks. "Oh, that has a bite."

She took a sip and relished the dryness of the cabernet. "It mellows out after a couple of sips."

"So the boxes? Are you heading out to Vegas?"

She shrugged, taking another sip of wine. "I haven't decided yet. Things with Calvin seem to be on a steady incline."

"You and the married guy?"

With a shift of discomfort, Leah chose to ignore his remark. "He has been very sweet and understanding."

"Leah, he's married. Nothing good can come out of it."

"He's separated and has suggested moving in together." She nibbled on a piece of sharp cheddar. "When that letter was left on my doorstep, Calvin couldn't have been more attentive."

"What letter?" She could detect a note of weary exasperation in his voice.

Without answering, she put her wine glass down and got up to retrieve the envelope from the top of the refrigerator. Handing it to him, she continued to nibble on her piece of cheese.

After reading the letter, Quincy folded it and placed it carefully back into the envelope. "Have you contacted the police?"

Leah shook her head. "No, this was a one-time incident. I don't want the police to waste precious time looking for a sociopath with a computer. They need to concentrate on finding Jason's killer." With another sip of wine, she muttered, "Not that they are really trying with his case anyway."

Quincy suddenly became aware of the large piano sitting in the middle of Leah's living room. "Now how could I have missed that? It takes up half your floor space."

She floated to the bench and placed her wine on the permanent coaster sitting on the piano. "Isn't it the most beautiful piano you have ever seen?" The hypnotic pull of music was ready to weave its harmonious spell over her.

"As far as pianos go, yeah, I guess you could say it is beautiful."

She could hear him shift on the couch. Her eyes remained fixed on the keys in front of her, visually pounding out a wild rhapsody.

"So what can you play?"

Mustering up every ounce of willpower, Leah finally pulled her eyes off the piano and onto her guest. "I play by ear, so if I've heard it, I can play it for the most part."

"Would you play something for me?"

She nodded slowly. "What would you like to hear?"

"I am a huge fan of the blues. Could you play something bluesy for me?"

"How about a little Duke Ellington?" She smiled, turning back to her most prized possession. Her fingers flexed over the black and white keys as she thought of the song she wanted. Moving slowly, the music began to fill the room, engulfing her into her own little world where nothing and no one could harm her...

The Bright Horizons Youth Group building was dark and empty when Leah and Jason came stumbling through his office doors giggling like a couple of teenagers.

"Don't scare me like that," she admonished with a smile. "It's not funny."

"You're right, I'm sorry." He laughed heartily. "But I just couldn't resist. Jumping out of that dark corner was too tempting."

"Do you think it has been long enough for the fish to acclimate to the aquarium?" she asked, tapping at the glass of the fish tank.

"Well, we went to dinner an hour ago." He untied the plastic bag and dumped the fish into the tank. They watched as the colorful creatures swam around, exploring their new environment.

"I can certainly see why fish are so calming." Leah smiled up at Jason.

He gestured without looking at her. "Which one is your favorite?"

Without hesitation, Leah picked an electric blue and yellow fish that seemed to glow brighter than the rest. "That one." She pointed.

"Then you need to name That One." He laughed.

"I am thinking Lily."

"Lily? Seems like an odd name for a fish."

"It was the first flower you ever gave me." She sighed wistfully.

"They are your favorite."

She felt his hand glide to the small of her back; the small circles his thumb drew sent a thrill up her spine. Leaning into him, she felt comfortable and safe. The words, "I love you" sprang to her lips, but she refused to utter them, choosing instead to bite down on her tongue so hard that tears formed in her eyes.

"Oh shoot, I forgot the fish food in the car." He kissed the top of her head. "Will you be okay by yourself? I'll only be a few minutes."

She nodded, avoiding his gaze. "Yep, I'll just keep myself busy watching the fish explore."

Jason kissed her lips quickly and disappeared out the door.

Leah looked around the darkened office and suddenly felt exhausted. Sinking into his office chair, her elbow bumped the mouse, which caused the monitor to awaken with a bright, jarring light.

After a few moments adjusting her eyes to the sudden glare, Leah noticed Jason's email had a new message.

"Let it go, Leah," she said quietly, her jealousy stoked into a slow burn. "Just because it is a woman's name..."

Before she could stop herself, her hand opened the email. With a thudding heart and jealousy moving from a simmer to a slow boil, she scanned the typed words.

Jason-

As much as I try to stay strong, sometimes my weakness gets the better of me.

I truly wish I didn't have to hide my feelings for you.

You are the first person I think of in the morning and the last person on my mind before I drift off to sleep and reunite in my dreams.

I can't help myself; I want you and only you.

The screen suddenly went dark. "What do you think you're doing?" Jason's hand hovered over the power button on the monitor.

"I-I-I was just..." Her face flushed with anger and embarrassment. Why did he get to be angry? He was in the wrong! Leah thought heatedly.

"Snooping. That's what you were doing," he continued.

"Who is she?" Leah asked boldly.

"Just a friend and none of your business."

"A friend does not write letters like that." Leah pointed at

the blank screen. "A friend does not say that she wants you and only you."

"I see her as just a friend and nothing more. I can't control how people feel about me."

Leah paused for a minute, trying to reel in her anger. He had a point, she thought. "Interesting, because you refer to me as a friend as well. Doesn't that put us on equal footing in your eyes? What happens when the next 'friend' comes along?"

He held up his hand. "You can stop right there. I don't call you my girlfriend because you know how much I hate labels." He slowly circled the desk. "You know how much I care for you, Leah, and how much commitment freaks me out, so cut me a little slack, please." He held out his hands to her. "You are special to me and no flowery email will change that."

And there it was, the smile. That perfect smile that made her heart thud and melt at the same time. Circling his arms around her waist, he pulled her in for a slow, sweet kiss that evaporated any negative emotion Leah had been feeling...

The clapping and whooping from Quincy pulled Leah back into reality with a jarring sense of absence. It took her a moment to remember Jason was dead and that his arms around her waist and his lips on her mouth were all a very vivid memory.

"That was amazing, Leah!" Quincy came over and settled himself on the bench next to her. "Get yourself to Vegas and play, girl!"

She self-consciously combed the fringe of hair at the base of her neck with her fingers. "Oh, you're just being polite."

"Uh, when have you ever known me to be polite?" Quincy laughed.

Leah soon joined in. "You're right." She nodded. "I just want to play." Her hand flew back to the fringes of her hairline. The glare of the monitor in that darkened office swam to the surface of her mind again. "Do you know of anyone named Cynthia or Cindy maybe?"

His face went through a rapid flicker of emotions that finally settled on confusion. "Can't say I do, but you know me, impolite and bad with names." He drained the last of his wine glass. "Why do you ask?"

She gave a little shrug. "No reason, just something I was

trying to remember."

Checking his watch, he sighed. "This has been great, but I really should get going. Early morning drills." He collected his coat. "And I'm not as young as I used to be."

"Thanks for stopping by." Leah wrapped her arms around his neck and pulled him close. "You have always been a good friend to me."

"I am always here for you," he said, squeezing her in return. "Remember that."

Rosa tapped her fingers impatiently on the steering wheel of her car. Checking her watch again, she glared at the one lit window in Bright Horizons. "Come on, Tanvir," she muttered, drumming out a senseless beat with her fingers. "Isn't it time for your nightcap?"

The man seemed so out of place compared to the rest of the team, Rosa never understood why Jason kept him around, but then Rosa felt dwelling on Tanvir was a waste of her time. He drank like a fish and didn't fit in anywhere.

Checking her watch again, she knew she was pushing her luck. Sneaking in past hours, lying to her mother so that she would watch little Jay-Jay, Rosa really hoped to find something to make the risk worth her while.

The light went out and Rosa breathed a sigh of relief. She watched Tanvir round the corner and walk out of sight before exiting her car and heading to the building. Her hand skimmed the inside of her purse for keys and a flashlight. *No use drawing attention to my snooping,* she thought as she fished out the items.

Stealthily making her way down the hall and into Jason's office, she wasn't sure where to start. Pulling on a pair of leather gloves, Rosa began methodically going through papers, searching for something, but not sure what. "I'll know when I find it," she muttered for reassurance as she opened up the first drawer and began to rifle through paperwork.

Rosa didn't want to be here any longer than was necessary. This was Jason's thing. He loved the thrill of the stress. No wonder he had visions of going into politics, she thought as she thumbed through a sheaf of papers. "Could be promising," she whispered, holding the papers she pulled out of the stack tight in her hand.

Opening up the bottom drawer, her thoughts were so wrapped up with Jason and Bright Horizons it took a moment for the words on the top page in her hand to penetrate her thought process.

"Oh my God!" she muttered sinking into the office chair. The rest of the papers fell to the floor. "Oh my God!"

Chapter Sixteen

Waking with a start, Calvin took several moments to remember where he was. He wasn't at home in his bed listening to the Saturday morning chaos in the kitchen. No smell of fresh coffee, no pancakes waiting for him.

The thought of food made his stomach growl angrily. Marla's pancakes would really hit the spot right now, he reflected. Tyler's serious voice was clear in Calvin's mind, reminding his mother not to butter his pancakes. It was always the same conversation and it made him chuckle to think his son didn't trust Marla enough to keep the butter off his pancakes.

Marla. Calvin missed sharing a bed with her. Even missed that annoying little snort thing she did when she slept. He felt depressed and lonely. What happened to his marriage, he wondered for the hundredth time, eyeing the sheaf of divorce papers on the end table. He was not ready to give up on his family. His wife, on the other hand, seemed to have a steely determination to end it.

A pang of regret and nostalgia hit Calvin as he laid on his friend's couch. "What am I doing?" He sighed, rubbing his eyes. It was Saturday morning and he had no plans with the kids. No fishing trip, no zoo excursion. Nothing. He wondered what they had planned for the day. Should he just pop over and say hi? See where the day took them? No, he realized with a sigh, better call first.

Picking up his cell phone off the floor, he hit the speed dial and waited. Calvin felt like a nervous teenager calling the girl he had a crush on. Marla's hurried hello came after the third ring.

"Hey," he answered, relieved to have caught her. "I wanted to see the kids this morning, didn't know what..."

Marla cut him off mid-sentence. "That would be great, Calvin, but we are spending the day with my folks at Fell Park. It is kids' day, a lot of stuff going on. Tyler and Pop-pop have plans to go to the new exhibit at the museum. Amanda wants to enter a jump rope contest."

He could hear his daughter's voice. "No, Mommy, I want to play hopscotch with Me-maw."

"Sorry, sweet pea." Marla laughed.

Calvin's heart constricted. He desperately wanted to be there to see the new museum exhibit, whatever it was, to cheer his daughter on, and to argue with his in-laws.

"I stand corrected," Marla said in that same rushed tone. "She and my mother will be having their own hopscotch competition."

"Oh and a balloon hat!" Amanda interrupted again. "I want a ladybug hat!"

"And a ladybug hat. We'll see if the balloon man is there."

"And popcorn!"

He could picture his daughter running around the living room, a whirlwind of excitement chanting about popcorn and ladybugs.

"What did you want, Calvin?" Marla asked quickly. "I am trying to get the kids out the door. We are running late this morning."

"Oh, uh," he stammered nervously. "I just wanted to stop by and see the kids this morning, but seeing that you have plans..."

"We'll be home probably around sixish if you want to stop by then. I am sure the kids would love to see you." He heard the note of finality in her voice. "Okay?"

"Yeah, sure." He nodded, trying to swallow the lump in his throat. "Six o'clock works great."

"Great, see you then, got to go." She hung up without a goodbye.

Calvin stared at the cell phone in his hand. An entire Saturday stretched before him and he had no idea what to do. He extracted himself from the sofa and wandered into the small kitchen to make some coffee. His stomach growled loudly again. Pancakes weighed heavily on his mind. He could go out to breakfast, but the idea of eating alone depressed him more.

Picking up the cell again, he punched in a series of numbers. "Hey, beautiful," he said when Leah answered the phone. "I was wondering if you had any plans for the day."

Leah tossed an apple in his direction. "Is this what you had in mind?" she asked with a laugh.

He caught the apple and bit into it, nodding. "The only expectation I had," he said after swallowing, "was spending time with you."

Adding a few more apples to their basket, she wandered to another tree. "My mother's birthday is coming up. I am going to make her some apple butter."

He looked at her quizzically. "Didn't I see jars of apple butter in the gift shop?"

Her giggling rang through the quiet orchard. "Yes, you did, but you haven't met my mother. She is a stickler for certain things. Homemade apple butter is one of them."

They wandered in amiable silence for a while. Calvin was determined not to let the mood from this morning ruin his day with Leah. She was smart, sexy, funny, and special. Jason was a moron for stringing her along like he did. Not appreciating what he had.

"After I got off the phone with you, I called Orchard Café and ordered us a picnic lunch." She interrupted his thought process. "I hope that is okay."

"It is definitely more than okay," he said, sliding an arm around her slender waist. They picked up their lunch and headed to a more secluded spot.

Calvin shook the blanket out and planned to lay it on the ground when he heard Leah tsk. "What?"

"I was thinking the hammock might be cozier." She pointed to the oversized netting strung between two large apple trees.

They situated themselves in the hammock and began to sway slowly. The quiet of the apple grove made their spot feel more secluded. Calvin pulled Leah closer, kissing the top of her head. "This is nice," he said with his eyes closed. His bare foot gently pushed them.

"It is." Her head nestled on his chest. She casually reached into the basket and pulled out a cracker. Dipping it into a container of soft cheese, she popped it into Calvin's mouth. "It is a perfect Saturday."

"Mmmm," he agreed, enjoying the lightness of her hand resting on his chest, feeling the rise and fall of her back under his own hand.

"I was thinking when we get back to my place, you might like to have dinner," she said gently. "I make a mean apple pie."

He pulled her closer. "Have to take a rain check. Have a date with my kids tonight."

"Well that is definitely more important than pie." Her body molded into his side.

His thumb skimmed the lightweight fabric of her blouse. It felt silky smooth. "Tomorrow?" He relished the languid flow of his afternoon.

"No, tomorrow I am going to visit Jason's mother."

He put an apple slice in his mouth and offered half to her.

Leah reached up and bit into the apple, kissing his lips softly. "Mmm, nice," she said, kissing him again.

"This was a good idea," he said as they snuggled back into the hammock, his bitter morning mood becoming a distant memory.

"Daddy!" Amanda rushed at her father, throwing herself in his arms. "Me-maw and I went hopscotching and jump roping and had cotton candy and popcorn and saw a puppet show and..."

"Whoa there, speedy!" Marla interrupted, "Give your father a chance to breathe. He just walked in the door!"

Calvin hugged his daughter tightly. "Ty?" he called out.

Tyler stepped out of the hallway. "Hey, Dad." He waved shyly.

"Hey, did you have a good day at the park today?"

His son nodded, bringing a package over. "Pop-pop got me this new dinosaur computer game."

"That looks like fun!" Calvin agreed, setting his daughter down on the ground. "Do you need help installing it?"

"Pop-pop got me a huge pink unicorn," Amanda chimed in.

Marla intervened. "Hey, Amanda, Daddy will read you stories for your special time, but right now it is Ty's turn."

"Awwww man!" She pouted, with a small stomp of her foot to protest.

"Bath time," Marla announced.

"Can I use your special bubbles?"

"You sure can," Marla said to her daughter's retreating figure. She cupped her son's face and gave him a wink. "Enjoy your game," she called over her shoulder.

Calvin appreciated his wife even more at that moment. Her ability to balance Amanda's boisterous behavior with Tyler's reserved nature. "Let's get to a computer." He threw his son over his shoulder and carried the giggling boy into the playroom.

About an hour later, his daughter, now finished with her bath and having a tea party with her dolls, reminded him it was her turn for his undivided attention. Swathed in her two favorite colors, red and purple, Amanda snuggled against her father, listening intently to the story she chose, *Ladybug Girl*. It was the same book she chose every night.

Calvin read quickly. He wanted a chance to spend time with Marla. Maybe they could talk and figure out how things got so bad between the two of them. His astute daughter, however, was onto him.

"This is my special time, Daddy, read slower and no more skipping words," she admonished.

He apologized and began the book again, reading at a normal pace. Amanda's breathing slowed and became more even. By the end of the book, she was barely conscious. Calvin kissed her good night and tucked her in. He checked in on Tyler who was sound asleep buried deep in the covers.

Tiptoeing into the kitchen, Calvin announced both kids were asleep.

"Thank goodness." Marla shook her head, pouring steaming tea into two mugs. "I am worn out! It's been a long day." She slid a mug across the counter to Calvin. "How was your day?"

A wave of guilt rolled through him as he remembered his sweet and uncomplicated afternoon with Leah. "Nothing special," he said with a wave of his hand, eager to change the subject. "How are your folks doing?" Calvin grabbed the honey and squeezed some into Marla's mug before he gave himself some.

"Ugh, the bickering seems to have gotten worse and it is always over little things." She stirred her tea slowly. "My mother changed the brand of travel Kleenex in her purse. My father acted as if she had a man stashed away in there. Apparently, it was a huge act of betrayal."

"Well, it kind of is," Calvin laughed. Marla's parents were nuts and it never ceased to amuse him the pettiness of their arguing.

She shot him a humorous look. "And how are *your* parents doing out in Siberia?"

"It is Alaska and my father thought it was a great piece of land."

"Three months out of the year," Marla laughed.

Calvin joined in the laughter. It was nice being on the same team after living as adversaries for so long. He reached over and touched her hand. The laughing abruptly stopped. Marla pulled away, leaning against the counter out of reach.

"It has been a long day." She sipped at her tea. "Those kids have way too much energy."

"Well you do a good job keeping up with them." He circled his finger around the rim of the mug. "You're a really good mother."

Marla tucked a lock of hair behind her ear, a clear sign she was uncomfortable. "Did you get a chance to read over the papers?"

Calvin's chest constricted. "No," he answered with a shake of his head. "I was too tired last night and..." He tried to formulate the words in his head. How much he missed his family, missed being home, how sorry he is for his role in the split. "Look, Marla..."

She pushed herself off the counter with a yawn. Calvin was pretty sure it was forced. "Oh, I am wiped! Amanda had me running ragged." She placed her mug next to the sink. "I am really looking forward to a hot bath."

"Why don't you let me do the dishes?" he offered, coming around to the sink. "While you are in the bath and when you are done, I can give you one of my world famous back massages." He knew he had gone too far the moment the offer left his lips.

It hung awkwardly in the air for a few moments before Marla regained her composure. "Why don't I show you out Calvin?" She faked another yawn. "I am going to lock up anyway. As soon as I am done bathing, I am crawling into bed." She opened the front door quickly and ushered him over the threshold. "Thanks for stopping by, the kids really appreciate seeing you. Night."

The door shut in his face and he heard the click of the lock being thrown. He touched the solid wood in front of him, wondering if they could ever get back to being on the same side of the door.

Marla leaned her forehead against the door with a sigh. Her emotions were in a tailspin, thoughts were reaching cyclone proportions. Was it possible to work things out? Could things really get better between them? She wondered.

A little voice in the back of her mind whispered, *What about the woman? Haven't we been through this before? Separation? Talk of divorce? He charmed his way back into your bed. It lasted, what? Three months? How is this any different?*

With shaky fingers, Marla entered the security code on the alarm system and set about turning off the lights, making sure windows were locked. *Does he still love me?* She couldn't be sure; Calvin could be really difficult to read sometimes. *Do I still love him?* She knew the answer was yes, as much as she hated to admit it.

Maybe if she had lost a few pounds or went blonde he would have remained interested. Adopting an alluring British accent maybe, as ludicrous as the thoughts were. She couldn't help but wonder, had she changed herself somehow, maybe they would still be together.

The bath was steaming and felt wonderful on her bare skin. As she sank lower into the hot sudsy water, immersion brought clarity to her confusing situation. She knew Calvin would never change. This was a never-ending pattern with him and she needed to keep her eyes wide open or else they would all end up right back where they started, together and miserable.

Chapter Seventeen

The interior of the Mini Cooper offered a bit of security for Leah as she nervously finger-combed the fringe of hair at the nape of her neck. "You are being ridiculous," she muttered, checking her reflection in the mirror. "They are warm, kind people."

Getting out of the car, she smoothed down her blouse and made her way to the oak front door. Her hand hovered a moment before she gave it a hard rapping. Waiting nervously, Leah shifted the apple pie from one hand to another and debated on knocking again when the door swung open.

An older woman bearing a remarkable resemblance to a modern day Donna Reed smiled brightly. "Why as I live and breathe." Her soft voice carried a deep southern drawl to it. "Leah, how are you dear?" She quickly stepped aside, signaling for the young woman to enter.

"Just fine, Mrs. Rowe." Leah stepped into the homey living room. "I hope you don't mind me just popping in like this."

"Not at all." The woman beamed. "Not at all! We love company!"

"I brought you a pie." Leah handed over the dessert.

Jason's mom took it with gratitude. "Oh my, aren't you just the sweetest thing." She put an arm around Leah's shoulder. "Come into the kitchen and have some breakfast. You look like you could use a bit of weight on your bones."

Entering the kitchen, Jason's mom continued. "Frank? Frank, look who's here."

"Leah!" Frank Rowe's face broke into a wide smile. Her chest constricted when she realized it was Jason's smile that she was seeing on his father's face. That charming smile that would get her to agree to anything.

"Frank." Mrs. Rowe stepped up to the stove, finishing up the final preparations for breakfast. "How many times have I asked you not to read the paper at the table?"

"I'm sorry, Gayle." He folded it up and laid it on the sideboard. "Paper is gone."

"Go wash up to eat, please." She handed Leah some dishes. "Be a dear and set these out."

Leah walked around the table, putting the plates down; her stomach gave an approving growl because of the aroma of the food.

They sat down and offered grace before eating. "So how are you doing?" Leah asked as she took a large, fluffy biscuit from the basket.

"Oh, we're getting by." Gayle smiled brightly. "How are you? We haven't seen you for ages." Her eyes lingered on the pie. "The pie smells wonderful."

"I went to Johnson's Orchard yesterday for fresh fruit. I wanted to make apple butter for my mother's birthday. I had several apples left over and thought you might like a pie."

"Oh, how sweet of you to put such an effort into your mother's birthday like that." Gayle took a sip of coffee. "It does a parent well when a child makes an effort." Her voice softened a bit more. "Jason used to bring that sweet little boy over for Sunday brunch every week after church." She dabbed at the corner of her eye. "He made an effort."

Frank cleared his throat loudly. "He was a good boy, despite what Rosa says."

"What?" Leah's head swiveled fast. "What did Rosa say?"

With a shrug, Gayle poured herself another cup of coffee. "We have not seen hide nor hair of her or our grandson since the funeral. Tried going over there and calling." She patted Leah's hand. "We all put forth an effort." She gave a sad shrug. "No luck. Rosa wants nothing to do with us."

"We decided to leave it in God's hands." Frank nodded sternly.

"Everyone grieves in their own way," Gayle said quietly. "Then she called the other night. Said she found something. A note." Two bright red spots appeared on her cheeks.

"Says my boy killed himself," Frank said with a hard edge to his voice.

Leah's head spun in confusion. "What? No! Not Jason!"

"I asked to see the note," Gayle said calmly. "I would know my baby's handwriting. She told me it was printed out on the computer."

"We raised our boy to be a man and take responsibility for his actions," Frank said.

The conversation seemed to fall flat after that. Leah wrestled with indignant rage for the blatant lie. Jason would never kill himself. He faced his problems head on. "I am sorry, I didn't mean to pry." She felt sad for taking part in this extremely private matter.

Gayle squeezed her hand. "I like you." Her smile was genuinely bright. "Out of all the girls Jason dated, you were my favorite. I told him to quit his running around and settle down with you." She laughed, lightening the air in the room. "He was certainly a charmer. Guess that comes with having three older sisters. He figured out very early on how to work his way into the female heart. I suspected Rosa would be trouble when we first met her," Gayle continued thoughtfully. "When she became pregnant, we were thrilled about the baby."

"Not so much with the mother," Frank said with a wry smile. "We assumed she was only after him for his money."

"But little Jay-Jay is such a sweet boy." Gayle's eyes lit up talking about her grandson. "Oh, I just love giving him hugs and listening to that giggle of his."

"Well, when he took up with that..." The conversation continued as if Leah wasn't in the room. "That woman..." Frank snapped his fingers. "What was her name? Cynthia? Samantha?"

"Oh yeah, Claudia." Gayle shuddered. "What is it they call an older woman who dates younger men? Tigers? Jaguars?""

Leah's mouth suddenly went dry. "Cougars?" The word barely left her mouth as she remembered the email she read in Jason's office. "They are called cougars."

"That's right, she was a cougar." Gayle shook her head. "A cougar pursuing my son."

"Who is Claudia?" Leah's question hung in the air unanswered as a thundering of feet came flying into the kitchen.

Two identical girls split at the door and each landed into a grandparent. Jason's sister, Julie, a stressed-looking woman, trailed in behind them. "Morning all!" She noticed Leah sitting at the table. "Hey, stranger!" Her smile beamed. Leah and Julie became friends when she was involved with Jason "How are you?"

"Just fine." Leah gathered her things together. "I really should get going."

Jason's mother situated her granddaughters at the table for breakfast. "Stay for another cup of coffee at least."

"I would love to, but I have an appointment." She kissed cheeks all around, gave Julie a comforting hug and vowed to stop by again soon.

Getting into her car, Leah decided she needed answers. Sneaking around wasn't getting her anywhere. She needed to go straight to the one person who could give them to her. She needed to talk to Rosa.

Where the insane idea to talk to Rosa came from Leah wasn't sure. As she made her way to Jason's house, her determination rose. Rosa was not the easiest woman in the world to talk to, let alone confront, but it had to be done.

Pulling up in front of the house, Leah found Rosa and little Jay-Jay watering flowers in the garden. Setting foot on the sidewalk, Leah's determination began to waver as Rosa glanced over at her. The look on the other woman's face made Leah want to drive as fast as she could away from the storm that was brewing in her eyes.

"Hi, Rosa!" She inwardly cringed at the amount of false enthusiasm her voice carried. "How are you today?" Boldly, Leah continued toward the front lawn, her wobbly legs threatening to give out at any minute.

"What do you want now?" Rosa sneered. "Didn't you find what you were looking for when you broke into my house?"

Leah tried to mask her shock. *How did she find out*? she wondered frantically. *This is insanity—get out! Get out now while you can!* But she stood her ground. "I need to talk to you, Rosa. I need to ask you..."

Rosa picked up the little boy. "Come on, Jay-Jay, let's go watch some cartoons."

He put his thumb in his mouth and watched Leah warily from over his mother's shoulder as she strode angrily into the house, slamming the front door behind them.

It only took a moment for Leah to decide. She had already rattled the hornet's nest, might as well shake it a little more. With purposeful strides, she made her way up the front steps and through the door. "Rosa?" she said calmly. "I really need to talk to you."

Rosa's eyes teemed with anger as she picked up her son and took him out of the room. She was back in a moment without him. "You will get out of my house before I call the police. I let your breaking and entering slide before. I will not hesitate to press charges this time."

"Not until I get some answers." Leah folded her arms stubbornly across her chest. "I want to see the letter."

"What letter?"

"The one you said you found. Jason's suicide note, I want to see it."

Rosa stepped past her and opened the door, her body shaking with rage. "You took Jason away from me." Leah saw her knuckles whiten grasping the doorknob. "You stole him from me and my son. You are nothing but a home wrecker and the least you can do is leave a widow to grieve in peace."

The words spurred Leah into a new fit of angry resolve as she reached over Rosa's head and shut the door. "When I see a grieving widow, I will pay my respects." She stood a good six inches taller than Rosa and stared her down. "Jason never married you. You are not a widow. You are nothing but a conniving, bitter woman who makes it her life's mission to make sure everyone around her is just as miserable." Shocked silence followed as Leah tried to maintain her composure. A flickering of emotions skittered across Rosa's face. "Now get me the letter," Leah said again, calmly.

"You have no idea how much I hate you, Leah. Jason was going to take my son away and leave me because of you!" Her eyes went wild, like a caged animal looking to find an escape. "Just leave us alone!" She wrenched the door open again. "Get out!"

"I didn't come here to argue with you, Rosa," Leah continued, hoping her false calm would penetrate the other woman. The last thing Leah wanted was for little Jay-Jay to witness this. "I came here to get some questions answered."

"Get out!" Rosa screamed. "Get out! Get out! *Get out of my house!*"

"Not until I see the letter."

Rosa broke down sobbing, covering her face with her hands. "I don't have it. I gave it to the police."

Her first instinct was to comfort Rosa, maybe even hug her. But Leah knew better and waited a moment before speaking. "I am sorry for any pain I may have caused." She waited a moment. "I never meant for anyone to get hurt."

The sobbing escalated. Leah wasn't sure if she should wait it out.

"Fine," she said over the crying. "I know we will never be friends. I know you will never forgive me for what I stole from you. But I just have one question."

Rosa's sobbing slowed considerably. Leah continued. "One question and I will leave you to lament over what you lost. I promise never to bother you again."

Hands slowly lowered from Rosa's face. Rage flashed in her eyes. "What?"

"Who is Claudia?"

Claudia assessed her appearance in the lit mirror on the vanity. She applied a thin veneer of concealer to her neck to hide a nasty age spot. The chimes from the grandfather clock downstairs informed her she needed to leave soon. Her husband would be calling up to her shortly.

The very thought of her husband doing anything caused a shiver of disgust to roll down her spine. A boring dinner, full of boring old people, discussing how very wonderful her dull husband was, was enough to make Claudia go screaming off to Europe for an extended vacation.

From a very early age, she knew how to turn any situation to her advantage. The more difficult the event, the more she wanted it, the harder she worked to succeed. After all, living in her family's successful shadow did little for her. She needed to stand out and show the world that she was more than a pretty face with a nice set of curves and bedroom eyes.

Bedroom eyes. The term made her giggle whenever she thought about it. How could someone have "bedroom eyes?" But that's what she had been told since she was fourteen. Claudia preferred the term seductive or sultry gaze. Although the term caused her a fit of giggles, it had proven to be most effective in wrapping men around her little finger to get what she wanted.

With a light coat of mascara and liner applied to her "bedroom eyes," Claudia assessed her appearance again before stepping into an original Valentino gown. The midnight blue silk complemented her creamy skin tone beautifully. Sliding on her favorite Louboutin heels, she turned in front of the full-length mirror, checking every angle, before declaring perfection.

"Claudia?" Her husband's voice drifted up to her from the foyer downstairs. Her teeth clamped together in irritation. "Are you almost ready?"

Choosing not to answer him, she walked into her closet and took her time selecting a bag to match her outfit from the shelves of clutches and purses she had accumulated. Life had been good to her. True, she chose to marry for position and power instead of for love, but what did it matter? Love left you vulnerable and weak. She had been there before and learned her lesson the hard way. Marrying a man who was in the position to support her in the manner she was raised seemed a much more advantageous prospect.

She had allowed herself a little crush. A little crush that quickly became an obsession. He didn't want to play by her rules, which made the game harder and therefore, more exciting. She wanted to be first in his world. He wouldn't put her on a pedestal. *Stubborn, stubborn man,* she thought with a touch of sadness. He was the only man to work his way into her heart.

She grabbed the clutch and her wrap and began to descend the stairs.

Her husband gave a low, approving whistle. "You look breathtaking, Claudia." He rested his hand on the small of her back and applied a little pressure. "You will be coming home with me tonight, right?"

Claudia had heard that tone before, it was one of warning. She knew how it bothered him that other men vied for her attention.

"Of course, darling," she said through a strained smile, walking faster to get his hand off her back.

Her dalliances were discreet. They had to be discreet. As much as she loathed her husband, she loathed the thought of losing her lifestyle more.

Younger men were much more pliable and much easier to manipulate. Fear was the perfect way to scare them, with her position, her power, and her ability to control their future. She likened herself to a puppet master, and Claudia enjoyed putting the fear of God into her pawns. Why risk everything she had worked for?

"Traffic is going to be a nightmare," her husband said, opening the car door for her.

She slid into the Mercedes. "It will be fine." The words were lost as he shut the door. Patting her perfectly coiffed hair, she looked herself over again in the mirror.

"You look lovely, now will you stop primping?" her husband said, sliding into the driver's seat.

Will you stop being such an oafish baboon? She bit her tongue hard. The question was sitting on her lips, begging to be released. "I just want to make sure your eye candy doesn't disappoint."

"Never seems to," he muttered, pulling out of the long driveway.

Claudia stared out the window. Her marriage was a sham. She knew it and her husband knew it. It has been years since they shared a bedroom, let alone a bed. She missed Jason immensely. The day her husband confronted her about their affair, she thought she had lost everything. Thankfully, she was able to backpedal and talk her way into his good graces.

But being in her husband's good graces wasn't going to bring Jason back to her.

Leah turned the business card over in her hand several times. Calvin had finally convinced her the night before to make the call. But he wasn't there to give her the final push. She lifted the phone, dialed six of the seven numbers, and hung up.

Taking a swig of coffee, she made herself push that seventh number and listened to the ringing of a distant phone.

"Homicide." The voice on the other end was gruff and unwelcoming.

Leah had a panicked lapse of silence.

"Hello?" the voice barked.

"Hi, Detective Becky, this is Leah. I am a friend of Jas...was...I was a friend of Jason Rowe's"

The silence stretched over the line. Leah opened her mouth to say hello before the detective answered.

"Oh right, okay—tall, leggy, long dark hair?"

"That would be me." Her nervous chuckle set her teeth on edge. "Am I catching you at a bad time?"

"Leah, every minute I work in homicide is a bad time."
The voice relaxed a little. "What can I do for you?"

"Um, well, I wanted to see how you were progressing
with the case. I, um, had this note stuck to my door and it
kind of unnerved me a bit. I didn't know if it was related to
the investigation?"

"Was it a threatening note?"

She read the note to the officer. "And I also heard that
Jason might have left a suicide note."

The derisive laugh on the other end startled Leah. "Oh
yeah, we got that. This was most definitely not a suicide. I
can run by later and pick up the note that was taped onto
your door, but to be quite honest, I don't think anything will
come of it." She heard paper shuffling on the other end of
the line. "Our trail has gone cold and we have no new leads.
So we were forced to close the case until we have something
solid to follow."

"So the case was closed?" A prickle of cold apprehension
ran over her. "You aren't pursuing it any longer?"

"Not until we get something concrete." The voice on the
other end softened a bit. "I'm sorry, Leah."

"Yeah." She felt a large wave of exhaustion roll over her.
"Yeah, I'm sorry too."

She hung up the phone and for the first time in years,
Leah was looking forward to visiting her parents and going to
church. She needed a bit of religious direction and spiritual
uplifting.

Answers still eluded her. Rosa was not the fount of information Leah hoped she would be. And now there is a new
person to talk to. Although it took a lot to go and talk to
Rosa, Leah knew that she would have to dig deeper to find
the courage to go and confront Claudia.

Chapter Nineteen

With her car streaming up the coastline, Leah marveled as the light of the rising sun streaked out across the sky in pinky-yellow hues.

"Absolutely gorgeous." She tried to remember the last time she was up to watch a sunrise. Dawn used to be her favorite time, when the sun just began to rise and cast new light on a fresh day.

Lately all she felt was apprehension, worry, and stress. This trip would be a good one for her, she decided. Good to get away. Give herself some space and prospective.

Her hand smoothed down the long skirt she wore. Leah took great pride in her appearance this morning, conservative black dress that fell well past her knees, cashmere cardigan to cover her arms, and light makeup. The only jewelry she wore was the small gold crucifix her parents gave her for her 16th birthday. "Don't want to show up to church looking like a Jezebel," she mumbled, turning onto the familiar road that would lead her home.

It was her mother's birthday and Leah had no intention of spoiling it. She spent years listening to her mother talk about the Jezebels that came to church with a face full of makeup and revealing too much skin. The least Leah could do was not cause her undue irritation.

As she made the final turn around the bend past the tall Myrtle trees, the church and parsonage came into view. The newly painted buildings shone in brilliant splendor, a beacon to those in need.

Leah parked in the little lot between the two buildings. Children's voices rose in an enthusiastic game of tag. An admonishing voice rose above the giggles, ordering the children not to play while in their Sunday clothes.

Leah resisted the urge to roll her eyes at the sounds of her childhood, Heaven forbid you have a ruffle get a smudge of dirt, or a pair of dress pants get torn. She did not know the woman who was reprimanding the children, but knew the lecture all too well.

"Leah?" Mr. Oliver, one of the deacons, approached her. He had shrunken with age, but his eyes still held a fervent intensity of an avid churchgoer. "Leah!" he said again, offering his hand in greeting, "How are you, my child?"

"Just fine, Mr. Oliver, thank you. How are you?"

"The Lord has blessed me," he nodded solemnly. "I suspect you are here to see your parents."

"I am." She smiled. "Is my mother seated already?"

He shook his head. "No, there are still a few minutes before the sermon. I believe they are still in the parsonage."

Leah headed to the parsonage next door. With a small rapping on the door, Leah held her breath, bracing for something, although she wasn't exactly sure what it was. The congregation next door began to sing. *"Only believe, only believe, all things are possible, if you only believe."*

"Leah?" Her mother's normally pinched face relaxed considerably. She gathered her daughter into a tight embrace as she cried out, "Thank you, Lord, thank you for bringing my dear child safely into your house of worship today."

Taken aback, Leah returned the hug. "It is good to see you too, Mother."

Her father appeared behind her mother. "The Lord answers all prayers." He thumped his worn Bible on his chest.

Leah realized he never seemed to age. He looked just as stoically handsome as he had when she was being chastised as a child for running around in her Sunday best.

"Hello, Father." She hugged him tight. "I've missed you."

"The Lord's grace and mercy keeps us," he replied.

"This is the best birthday present a mother could ask for." Her mother clasped her hands together in front of her.

"We must be going." He gestured to the door.

The singing from the congregation seemed to have doubled in its loudness since she had entered the parsonage, Leah thought. *"Lord I believe, Lord I believe, all things are possible, Lord I believe..."*

They had started across the lawn toward the church when her father squeezed her elbow gently. "Leah? Would you mind going on ahead and playing for us as we enter?"

"That is a splendid idea!" Her mother clutched her Bible tighter. "I miss seeing your face behind the piano during services."

Leah quickly walked across the lawn, through the back door, up the small stairway, and into the sanctuary. The congregation had just been seated. She spotted some familiar faces, others were new. Mrs. Darby was seated at the piano Leah had spent so many hours playing. She tried to get the old woman's attention subtly.

Mrs. Darby's eyes lit up with recognition. "Leah!" she whispered loudly. The congregation turned to who the person was sneaking around the pulpit.

The woman scrambled off the bench and shuffled down the steps to an empty spot in the front pew. Leah stood uncertain as whispering and gestures rippled through the congregation. With a deep breath, she sat at the familiar piano and began to play her mother's favorite *Under Your Wings* by Claude.

She looked up to watch her parents beaming in the back of the church, ready to make their weekly procession up to the pulpit. So many services she sat there, playing, singing for the congregation—for her parents. This building, these people, was her roots.

Her father gave an approving nod as he took his seat on the dais, the large, ornate wooden throne he had occupied for years.

The music was in her and it made all her problems so insignificant. Calvin was a distant thought. She no longer feared Claudia. Jason was a beautiful memory.

All her troubles washed away with the music. The music was in her, it was who she was.

"It is so good to have you home." Her mother passed a bowl of green beans to her father. "And the apple butter is wonderful, thank you."

"Everyone in the congregation raved about the music you played." Her father ate a forkful of mashed potatoes.

"That is very kind of them," Leah said, poking her food with her fork. Sunday dinners rarely varied. Her mother would start the pot roast before services so that after church they could all sit down to have the family meal. When the meal was over, it was off to Bible study.

Leah knew she needed to tell them about what she had been wrestling with, but couldn't seem to form the words. "I have been practicing my music quite a bit," she offered with a weak smile. "I am thinking of giving up event planning and playing piano...professionally."

Her mother shook her head reproachfully, "Music is not what a proper Christian should be pursuing."

"I understand your concerns, Mother, but..." Leah said lightly.

"Do not speak to your mother in that tone," her father warned quietly. He put his fork down and picked up the glass beside his plate. After taking a drink of water, he carefully wiped his mouth with his napkin. "Leah, we think it best if you did something with your college education. Music is a hobby and a very unstable source of income."

"But I love music so much!" She tried to keep her tone light, conversational. The last thing she wanted was an argument or to be regarded as a petulant child. "I just want to pursue something I love."

"You can play for the church," her mother said happily. "Mrs. Darby wouldn't mind giving you your seat back. Her arthritis is getting so bad."

"God has a plan for your life." Her father picked up his fork, a clear sign the matter had been dropped. "Follow your heart and we will continue to pray for you."

Once dinner was over, Leah offered her goodbyes with promises to visit again soon.

"May God be with you," her mother said from the front porch as Leah got into her car and started to drive away.

While Leah continued down the coastline, a little of the euphoria she had felt earlier had ebbed. She missed Calvin. Maybe she should invite him over for dinner tomorrow night.

And then there was Claudia. She grimaced at the thought of talking to her. How was she going to approach her? The gala would be an easy enough place, but she needed to talk to the woman in private.

The muffled ringing of her cell phone distracted Leah from thoughts of Claudia. Digging out her phone from under her coat and purse, she quickly answered it before it went to voicemail.

"Leah, where are you?" The voice sounded hurried.

"Quincy? Is that you? You sound weird. Are you okay?"

His breathing came heavier across the line. "There has been another incident at the office."

"Uh oh! Did the seating chart for the gala get misplaced?" Her giggles died down when she realized she was the only one laughing. The silence stretched on. "Quincy? What is it? You're kind of scaring me."

"It's Tanvir," he said quickly. "He's been attacked and is in a coma."

Leah's heart raced with fear. "Oh my God!" She jerked her car to the left to avoid going into a ditch. "I'm driving now. What hospital is he at?"

Once Quincy told her, she said she would see him there. Without a goodbye, Leah hung up the phone, gripped the steering wheel tighter, and pressed down on the accelerator.

"Yes, may God be with me," Leah whispered to herself.

Chapter Twenty

Leah pulled into the hospital parking lot and spotted Calvin sitting on a bench just outside the entrance. Relief flooded through her to see him waiting.

"Thank you so much for meeting me," she said, coming over to him.

He pulled her close. "It was the least I could do." His arms circled around her. "How are you holding up? You must be exhausted from being on the road."

With a shaky breath, she answered, "I'm doing fine." Glancing at her watch, Leah stepped back. "Visiting hours is almost over."

Hand in hand, they made their way to Tanvir's room. As they approached the closed door, arguing was heard from inside his room; although the voices were distinguishable, the words were not. The closer they got, the quieter the argument became. As Leah opened the door, she found Coach Turner staring at a football game. Quincy had his back to them, staring out the window.

Tanvir laid prone on the hospital bed; his tanned skin looked sallow against the stark white sheets. The monitors continued their beeping and the intubation machine offered a reassuring whoosh with every breath it gave Tanvir.

Squeezing Calvin's hand for reassurance, Leah walked into the room. "Quincy?" she said quietly.

Coach Turner was the first to answer. "Hi, Leah." His face held a kind of weary acceptance to the status quo. His eyes flickered to Calvin. A look of confusion crossed his face before it went back to the impassive look. Coach gestured to the chair next to him.

Quincy turned to face Leah. "Hey, thanks for coming."

Instinct took over as Leah gathered Quincy into a hug. "Are you okay?" she asked with a squeeze.

Breaking the embrace, Quincy took a step back. "Yeah," he said with a cracked voice. Taking her hand, he said with little confidence, "Yeah, I'm okay."

Leah took Tanvir's hand in her free one. "What did the doctors say?"

"Well." Quincy rubbed the back of his neck. "He has massive bruising around his head and neck. There is a brain bleed, but the doctors can't do anything about the bleed until the swelling in his brain goes down."

"What? We just sit and wait?"

Quincy nodded slowly. "We just sit and wait." He let go of Leah's hand. "I called his family in London. They were going to catch the first flight they could."

"What do the police say? Do they have any leads?" Fear prickled her spine.

"This is bad," Quincy answered. "This is bad, bad publicity. This is bad for the organization." He took a shuddering breath. "I really can't lose another friend right now. First Jason and now...this is bad."

"Excuse me?" The nurse said from the door. "But visiting hours are over. I will have to ask you all to leave."

They filed out of the room slowly, quietly saying their goodbyes to Tanvir.

Outside, the moon cast a silver glow across the dark parking lot. It contrasted oddly with the artificial glow of the orange outdoor lights. Leah contemplated the differences in color as the sliding glass doors opened. When she stepped over the threshold, Leah expected the cool night air to wash over her. Instead, she walked into a thick cloud of cigarette smoke. She coughed and sputtered, trying to see who was polluting her air space.

"Sorry," the familiar face said with a derisive chuckle. "I am stressed. I smoke when I am stressed." Her scarlet lips parted in a passable smile. The cigarette was thrown onto the ground and squashed like a bug.

It took a moment for Leah to tear herself away from the woman's glittering eyes.

The woman quickly lit another one. "How is he?" she asked casually, as if she were inquiring about the weather, exhaling a steady stream at the foursome.

"No change," Quincy muttered, scuffing the ground with his big toe.

Leah's stomach turned with nausea. Her body vibrated with nervous apprehension. Calvin stepped closer, sliding his hand around her waist. She felt a bit more secure with him standing close.

The jingling of keys pulled her back into the moment. "Come on, honey." Coach pulled out his keys. "It has been a long day. Let's go home."

The smoldering cigarette was squashed like the first one. "You go," Mrs. Turner said, her tone never faltering from flat and businesslike. She cinched her black Helmut Lang raincoat closed. "Quincy will take me home." She walked briskly past her husband. "There is still a lot of work to do before the gala." Quincy opened his car door. "Don't wait up," she said before sliding into the Lexus.

They watched as the car drove off into the night.

Rage flashed across the coach's face before he slid into his Mercedes. Leah and Calvin watched as he tore out of the parking lot.

"Oh, that was a little intense," Calvin said quietly once the roar of the engine died down.

Leah rubbed her arms roughly. She could not contain the irritation she felt. If she couldn't speak to Claudia Turner in a hospital parking lot, when would she ever find the courage to talk to her? Why was she so intimidated by the woman?

Leah finally reasoned it just wasn't the time to talk. Tanvir was fighting for his life for God's sake. Why would she want to confront anyone at a hospital?

"Did you want to come over?" Leah kept her eyes fixed ahead at the parked cars.

"I wish I could, but I promised the kids I would tuck them in tonight." He looked at his watch. "I am already running late."

"Oh," Leah said with concern. "Go, go. I can get home on my own." She gave him a quick kiss. "Go be with your kids."

"I will call you later." Calvin pulled her in for a lengthier kiss.

After Calvin left her, Leah climbed into her car. As exhausted as she was, she couldn't bring herself to go home. She drove around and found herself at the Bright Horizons building. The darkened windows looked ominous looming in the silver moonlight. She thought it was odd. If Claudia and

Quincy were working, why were there no lights on?

Leah drove her car over to Quincy's house and pulled to a stop. The small brick structure only had one window lit. Through the bay window, Leah could see them kissing and pawing each other. They disappeared from view and a light appeared in another room. Two shadowy figures behind a curtain appeared to be kissing and undressing each other before the lights went out again.

Leah started her car and inched away from the curb. She passed a dark Mercedes sitting across the street from Quincy's house. Leah recognized the car, her palms began to sweat, and she gripped the wheel so hard her knuckles turned white.

After tossing and turning for the better part of an hour, Leah finally gave up trying to sleep and made herself some tea. Flipping on the TV, she surfed through channels but could not get the shadowy image out of her head.

Landing on the tail end of a romantic comedy, Leah watched as the man professed his undying devotion to the woman he loved, asking her to marry him. She answered with a teary yes. They kissed, they hugged, they laughed, and confetti rained down upon them. It wasn't this difficult in the movies, Leah thought. Why did life have to be so hard?

There was nothing on television to hold her interest. Leah pulled out her laptop and opened it up. "Might as well figure out where I am going to move," she sighed.

An old picture popped up to greet her. It was of her and her father when she was five. They were sitting on the steps of the church smiling. Her father looked so—content.

The words he spoke to her earlier that day resonated through her. *Follow your heart, Leah.*

"Follow your heart, Leah," she said out loud.

Maybe she didn't have the courage to speak with Claudia that night, but she found a renewed sense of confidence—of following her heart—as her fingers flew over the keyboard, searching airline flights.

Pulling the news clipping she had saved out from under a small box on her end table, Leah made up her mind.

She was going to Vegas.

Chapter Twenty-One

Claudia pulled out her keys and gave Quincy a little finger wave. She waited until his car disappeared down the driveway before slipping into the house. It was quiet, a very welcome quiet.

Exhaustion washed over her as she leaned up against the door. She was glad the lights were off and there was no husband waiting to greet her. The last thing she needed was a confrontation.

Slipping blue suede pumps off her aching feet, she headed toward the stairs.

"It's about time," the voice slurred from the dark.

Claudia shrank at the sound. Squinting into the darkness, she saw her husband sitting in a wingback chair, the dying fire casting an eerie glow across his strong face. "Do you realize it is almost two in the morning?" His voice took on a menacing tone that Claudia had only heard a handful of times before. The tone was brought on by too much scotch, and insecurity.

"It *is* two in the morning," she replied coolly, eyeing the crystal scotch glass in his hand, wondering how much he had consumed. "And if you don't mind, it has been a long evening." She continued on her path to the stairs.

"Work hard, did you?" His tone shifted from menacing to patronizing, a sure sign he was about to blow. Claudia tried to think fast, to come up with the quickest escape route.

She attempted a bored sigh. "The gala is looming and nothing is going according to plan."

"Do you think I am an idiot?" he asked quietly, slowly rising from his chair. "Do you think I believe that load of crap you are shoveling at me?"

Claudia recoiled from the image of his words. "I have no

idea what you are talking about." The crystal glass was hurled through the air. Claudia moved her head just in time; it shattered on the wall behind her. "You idiot! That was a gift I received from Italy! They are irreplaceable!"

"Oh, I'm sorry. Was it a gift from your precious *Jason*?" He closed the gap between them. "Or one of your other play things?"

She turned, hoping to get up the steps before he reached her. "No, from my brother, you jealous old..." Claudia was pulled by her hair from the second step. Her husband's fingers circled through her blonde strands and held tight, pulling her close.

Fear gripped her as she realized he had gone over the edge. The wild-eyed look in his eyes held nothing of the sane man the university honored. Claudia's stomach clenched as she inhaled the strong stench of alcohol. Out of the corner of her eyes, she saw a fist raise.

"Hit me, you worthless buffoon." She could hear the taunting and could not stop herself. "You better have a mighty good explanation for my brother and everyone else at the gala on why I look like a punching bag."

The fist shook and fell back to his waist. Fingers released their hold on her hair.

"That's what I thought," she said, trying to keep her panic from showing. "Now if you will excuse me, I am going to my room." Claudia turned and walked on shaky legs up the stairs.

"Quincy is a fool for getting wrapped up with the likes of you," her husband slurred. Claudia froze on the step. "If he's not careful, he will end up dead just like your darling Jason."

She heard his heavy footfalls retreat across the foyer. The slam of the door to the study spurred her up the stairs and into her bedroom. With the door bolted, Claudia slid her vanity chair under the door knob just to be safe.

Alone at last, Claudia took a moment to catch her breath and realize she was safe. The adrenaline she felt a moment ago was replaced by exhaustion. Stretching herself across the bed, she was asleep before her head hit the pillow...

"Jason?" Claudia perched herself on the edge of his desk. She inched her skirt just a bit higher before touching his arm. "Why are you so tense today?"

"Trying to get some work done," he said, not looking up from the monitor. "Have to be out of here on time tonight."

He turned his arm as if to knock a bug off his skin. "What do you want, Claudia?"

"Spending time with Leah, I suppose?" She tried to keep the disappointment out of her voice.

Jason continued working as if she hadn't said anything.

"Nice aquarium. It goes well with your décor. Did Rosa get that for you?"

"No, Leah and I put it together the other night." Jason's eyes remained fixed on the computer, his fingers furiously inputting information into the system.

Claudia clucked her tongue playfully. "You are such a player, Jason. You must really enjoy the pleasure you get from all these women fawning over you." She waited for a reaction and got nothing in return. He was too busy working. She inched a little closer and leaned into him. "How is Rosa?"

He shrugged. "I don't know, haven't talked to her recently."

She could tell he was getting annoyed. Claudia got off the desk and went to the back of his chair. Her fingers dug into his tense shoulders.

"You must have slept with her by now," she continued, rubbing his shoulders and running her hands down his arms. "I mean, you have known her now for what? A few months?"

"I think she may have slept over once or twice." He gently shrugged her off of him. "I can't be sure."

Claudia perched herself on the sturdy arm of his executive chair. "Well, if you can't remember, it must not have been very good." She fiddled with the top button of her blouse. "I am sure poor Leah would be devastated if she knew about Rosa." The button "accidentally" popped open, revealing the lacy edge of a black bra. "And how you two met at that nightclub." She leaned in closer, waiting for him to turn away from his computer. "Does Leah know about the nightclub?"

"What about Leah?" Jason asked. He turned quickly in her direction and back to his computer.

"I asked if she knew about Rosa and your nightclubbing," Claudia asked.

"No, Rosa is just someone I hooked up with a couple times when Leah and I were on the outs."

Claudia slid the toe of her shoe casually up Jason's pant leg. "There is no need to lie to me," she purred. "We both know you are playing those two naïve girls like a fiddle." She slid her arm across his shoulders. "You need a woman who won't let you get away with such antics."

She put her lips up to his ear. "Did you get the email I sent the other night?"

Jason bolted out of his chair. "Claudia, please, I am really busy right now and in about two minutes I have a meeting with..."

The office door opened up. "Hey, Jason, I thought we could start our meeting early." Coach looked up from his notes. "Am I interrupting something?"

Claudia felt her face flush with anger and embarrassment. "No, dear, we are finished here." She stood casually, keeping her tone and body all business. "Jason, I will follow up with the fundraising committee." Gathering a couple files off the desk, she continued. "And I'll get you the figures for running an extended summer basketball camp." She inched past her husband, but caught the look in his eye. He was on to her and her infatuation. Claudia would have to be extra careful in this situation.

Closing the door firmly behind her, Claudia tried to look casual, standing in the hall as she listened at the doorway for a snippet of conversation. She didn't have to wait long before her husband's gruff voice pushed its way through the door. "What is going on with you and my wife?"

Claudia sat bolt upright in bed. She looked frantically around wondering what it was that woke her. The door was still bolted, the chair firmly in place. Nothing was amiss. A soft tapping of branches against her window eased her panic. It was the wind, she concluded, laying back down onto her bed. Her body felt heavy with the weight of clothing. The previous evening came rushing back to her in startling clarity. Quincy. Her husband. A new wave of fear washed over her. How much did her husband actually know?

Quincy was handsome and talented, but he definitely was no Jason.

"Jason," she whispered. A tear escaped from the corner of her eye. She loved him so much and wanted him so badly. But Jason refused to give her his heart. Leah and Rosa wanted him too. It all became too complicated.

Jason. Claudia couldn't help but love him. And now, because of what they built together, he was dead.

Chapter Twenty-Two

As the plane circled the night sky, Leah glanced out of the small window. Her lungs expanded with a sharp intake of breath. Far below her were the glowing lights of the Las Vegas Strip. The collective excitement among the passengers in the cabin intensified as the captain announced their descent into the city of lights.

Nervous anticipation washed over her as Leah gripped the armrests. She was really doing it; she was here and really doing it!

The plane began to lower itself, the lights became brighter, larger, and her nervous anticipation grew into an anxious panic. Was she ready to make this leap? Was she good enough to audition for a major show? What if she was asked to read sheet music? She could read music, but it took her several minutes to decipher the notes, and if she was this nervous...

STOP IT! Her voice of reason finally shouted. *Stop it! You need to try this or else you will never know.* Leah exhaled slowly, releasing some of the negative thoughts clouding her judgment. *Follow your dream, follow your heart, this is it. If it doesn't work out then you will be upset but will move on.* Leah did another slow exhale; her nerves calmed a bit more. *How do you know if you don't try?*

As the wheels hit the pavement, Leah released her death grip on the arm rests. She was here in Vegas for two days only to audition and search for a place to live—just in case. Just in case she actually got lucky in Vegas and landed the gig, but first she had to roll the dice and see. Passengers jostled themselves into a line to leave the plane.

Animated chatter surrounded her as she tried to get into

the line. A man offered her a place in front of him. She gave a small smile by way of thanks and dug into her purse for her cell phone, which began to ring and vibrate as soon as she turned it on. Quickly silencing it, she saw that it was Calvin calling. A slight sense of guilt tapped at her with the small lie she told him. He had no idea she was in Vegas. Calvin thought she was home, apartment hunting, job hunting. Leah did not want to say anything to him until there was something to say.

The line began to widen, which gave Leah a bit more breathing room once they filed into the terminal. Following the signs to baggage claim, she could sense the man still behind her. Leah quickened her step. The sooner she got her suitcase, the sooner she could get to the hotel. A hot shower and a late night snack would be wonderful. Maybe even a stroll along the strip.

"Is this your first time in Vegas?" A voice broke into her thoughts.

Turning her head, she found the man standing next to her. She gave him another smile and discreetly stepped away, searching for her suitcase.

"This is my first time in Vegas. I'm from Rockland, Maine."

Leah offered him a slight nod to let him know she heard him, but was not offering anything in return. Making friends was not on her agenda. She needed to concentrate on the audition and take a much needed break from the drama at home.

"I am looking forward to a change of scenery," he said.

She gave another nod as she saw her hideous flowered suitcase. It was easily visible since she had never seen another piece of luggage splotched in orange, brown, pink, and green.

"Is that yours?" The man reached the belt before she did. "Let me get that for you." He pulled her suitcase to the floor.

"Thank you," she said curtly, taking the handle from him. "It has wheels." Without another word, she wheeled her ugly suitcase out into the balmy Vegas night.

"Taxi!" she called, raising a hand. Yellow, green, red cabs all whizzed past her and picked up passengers to the left and right of her. "What, am I invisible?" she asked quietly as she tried to hail another cab.

Pulling out her guidebook, she wondered if there was a shuttle she could take to the hotel.

A cab pulled up in front of the man who seemed to be

stalking her. "Where to?" the driver asked gruffly.

"Take the lady first." The voice was becoming all too familiar. "She's been waiting awhile." He offered her a smile.

"No, that's okay. It's your cab." She stepped aside.

"I can wait for another one. You go. I insist." His smile was nicely set into a defined square-cut jaw. Hazel green eyes were prominently displayed above a nose that some would consider large, but Leah thought it suited his features.

"I'm sure the hotel has a shuttle. I'm going to the Hilton."

"So am I!" he said, coming forward.

A horn blast from the driver interrupted them. "Either someone get into the cab or close the door so that I can find a fare that actually wants to go somewhere," he yelled.

"We'll share the cab," Leah decided. He might be a stalker, but Leah felt relatively certain that she would be safe in the cab. "Split the fare."

He grabbed her suitcase, threw their luggage into the trunk, and climbed into the back seat after Leah.

"Just so you know," the cab driver warned as he pulled into traffic, "I started the meter when I stopped to pick you up. That whole three minutes of arguing you did is on you. I don't get paid waiting around for people to make up their minds. Time is money, after all."

Leah caught the man's eyes and they burst into laughter.

"Not used to taxis in Maine. This is a whole new experience for me." Quiet serenity seemed to radiate from the man's face. "My name is Austin, by the way."

Turning her face to the window, she fiddled with the pendant around her neck, soaking up the scenery around the Vegas strip, avoiding a return answer. "The lights are so bright! It's like noon outside."

"This should be called the city that never sleeps," Austin said, looking out on his side.

The cab pulled to a jerky stop in front of the Hilton. Austin had money in his hand before Leah could pull out her wallet. "It's on me, thanks for sharing the ride." Austin paid the cab driver and retrieved the luggage from the trunk.

"So, uh, Miss, what brings you to Vegas?"

Leah took her suitcase from him. "Business," she answered vaguely. Her phone began to ring again. She knew it was Calvin, but didn't have the energy to talk with him. "It was nice to meet you, Austin," she said as she headed to the front desk.

Room key in hand, Leah stepped off the elevator and saw Austin halfway down the hall.

"We really should stop meeting like this," he laughed.

"You stalkers are all alike." She smiled at the irony of this man being one step ahead of her since they landed. Leah turned away and headed down the hall, looking for her room number.

"Maybe I wouldn't have to stalk if I knew your name," he called after her.

"Guess I'll be seeing a lot more of you then, huh?" She entered her room and shut the door firmly behind her.

After a steaming hot shower, Leah was in need of some food. Throwing on an old comfortable college T-shirt and faded blue jeans, she slipped her feet into a pair of worn sandals and headed out to the elevators.

Stepping into the lobby, with the chaos of the casino and the brightness of the lights, Leah had to check her watch to remember it was ten o'clock at night. She saw Austin across the room and ducked her head to avoid eye contact. She almost made it to the door before he caught up with her.

"Hey, where you headed off to?" he asked eagerly.

She shrugged. "I am taking a short walk down the strip before I turn in for the night. Nothing exciting."

"Let me join you." He fell into step next to her outside. "There is too much excitement in the air to sleep and I just need to work off this nervous energy." He shoved his hands into his pockets and they walked together quietly. "So what business are you in? That brings you out to Vegas?"

Leah wrestled with herself. She had no intention of forming any kind of acquaintance, but Austin was just too likable to ignore. "I am a pianist," she said with a resigned sigh. "I am here for an audition."

He stopped abruptly. "Don't toy with me!" he said, pulling her arm.

"What?" She tried to keep her sarcasm in check. "You have a thing for piano players?" Maybe he wasn't as likable as she thought.

"No, I am a piano player auditioning for the new show

over in the..."

"Bellagio?" they said together.

Leah suddenly felt very comfortable with this man. "I was actually looking for a bite to eat. I am starving. Would you like to join me?"

"Only if you tell me your name." He smiled.

"It's Leah." She offered her hand. "My name is Leah."

The loud ringtone of her phone caused Leah to sit bolt upright. Her hand reached for her phone. "Ugh, forgot to call Calvin last night." She yawned and headed to the bathroom before answering her phone

"Leah?" Calvin didn't wait for the perfunctory hello. "What is going on? Are you okay? I tried calling you several times last night."

"And hello to you too," she grumbled, running a brush through her hair.

"Well, I'm sorry, but it isn't like you to not answer your phone or return the dozen messages I left for you."

Leah took the phone away from her ear and squinted at the screen. It read she had 13 messages. "I am fine," she said, trying to hide the fact that she was brushing her teeth. "I have just been really busy."

The evening with Austin flew by as they talked about music and life. Leah discovered he was a professional pianist who had played in all the major markets except Vegas. Her negative attitude began to whisper in her ear wondering if she was ready or if she was going to make a fool of herself.

"Oh," Calvin said, bringing her back into the present. "Okay, well, I was wondering if you wanted to go get some breakfast this morning?"

Leah had a fresh shirt barely over her head when there was a knock at her door. "I would love to, Calvin." She pulled on a skirt. "But my morning is packed with appointments." Pulling on her boots, she continued. "I will call you later and we can set something up for later on in the week?"

"Yeah, sure." He sounded sad.

Leah felt bad for lying to him. "I have to go. I'll talk to you later." She didn't wait for a goodbye as she hung up the phone and opened up the door.

"Good morning, Austin." She smiled brightly.

Chapter Twenty-Three

The opulence of the Bellagio lobby made Leah feel small and insignificant. Adjusting her shirt self-consciously, she tried not to stare at the surgically enhanced woman strutting across the floor.

A seemingly wealthy gentleman entertained two women, one on each arm. All three were dressed as if they were heading out for a fabulous evening. Leah wondered if they were aware it was eleven in the morning.

Her mother's disapproving tsk whispered in her ear. "Money is the root of all evil." Leah tried to ignore it, but there was another tsk waiting. "'Tis easier to pass through the eye of a needle than for a rich man to enter the kingdom of heaven."

One of the women wore a sequined red cocktail dress, her blonde hair rolled in an elegant chignon. She reminded Leah of Claudia. A small pang of anxiety hit as she thought of home. "Stay focused," she whispered to herself. "Concentrate on the music."

"Did you say something?" Austin asked, guiding her out of the flow of traffic.

"Pep talk," she said quietly, afraid that anything above a whisper would disrupt the ambience of the Bellagio.

Looking around, he pointed to a gold plated sign. "The Tower Ballroom is this way." Leading her to the left, he leaned in and spoke quietly. "Auditions always make me nauseous."

She gave him a dubious look. "You don't look nauseous."

"I hide it very well." They stopped in front of a long table. "We are here for the auditions," he said to the bored woman across the table.

"Fill out the forms in full and bring them back to me to get a call number." The woman handed over two clipboards without looking up from her book.

Piano music wound its way through the doors and rattled Leah's nerves. "It's about the music," she muttered, filling out the paperwork. "Remember the music." The tremor in her hand shook the pen she was using.

Austin laid a calming touch upon her arm. "You will be fine," he said with an easy smile. "Take a deep breath and imagine everyone in their underwear."

Leah burst out laughing. "Oh great! Thanks! That's all I need in my head."

He joined in the laughter. "If it gets you to stop talking to yourself, then I consider it a success."

They turned in the forms and received their number. Leah pinned the red 49 to her shirt and patted her stomach.

"Ready?" Austin asked, gesturing to the doorway.

Giving a nod, she walked into the ballroom and stopped short. There were people milling around chatting easily. A long table with several people sat in front of a gleaming piano. She marveled at the sheen of the wood and wondered how many hours of polishing it took to achieve such a brilliant shine.

"I need to sit down." Leah felt short of breath.

Austin led her to a row of chairs. "Sit. I'll be right back."

She sank into a chair and closed her eyes, taking several cleansing breaths to keep the impending anxiety attack at bay.

"Do you need a paper bag?"

Her eyes flew open at the sound of the voice. It took all of Leah's effort to zero in on the pale, freckled skin of the woman sitting next to her.

"You look a little sick." The woman snapped her gum between her teeth. "Too bad you're stuck in here. It's gorgeous outside." She turned back to her magazine and flipped a page. "You look like you could use some fresh air." She flipped another page, looking bored. "I could use some fresh air. Have you seen Red Rock Canyon?"

"What?" Leah asked. The woman's red hair seemed to circle her head like a fiery halo.

"Red Rock Canyon. It is amazing out there." She didn't look up from her magazine. "I am going hiking as soon as this audition is over."

Leah caught sight of Austin striding purposefully across the room. She admired his calm, self-confident demeanor and decided that was something she would aspire to. The sweaty, anxious pianist she was at the moment didn't sit well with her.

"Here." Austin handed her a bottle of water. "Drink this and eat some of these." He passed Leah a package of peanut butter crackers. "You'll feel better."

The woman next to her lost all interest in the magazine.

"Hello!" she said to Austin. "Are you here to audition? My name is Tabitha. Tabitha McCauley." Her hand reached across Leah's face to Austin.

"Austin Winter." He shook her hand quickly and paused before asking, "McCauley? Are you related to Clark McCauley?"

Tabitha nodded her head. "He is my uncle."

Austin looked around. Leah felt there was something more to this, but had no idea who Clark McCauley was.

"Are you here to audition?" Austin asked slowly. "Or just observing." The smile he offered seemed to ease the obviously loaded question.

Tabitha's cheeks tinted pink. "Both, I suppose." She answered quietly and then her voice brightened. "Hey, have you ever been to Red Rock Canyon? I am going there after these auditions. It is a perfect day for hiking."

Looking over Tabitha's attire, Leah couldn't help but be a little critical. The woman wore torn faded blue jeans and a lacy camisole under an oversized flannel. She seemed a little underdressed for an audition.

"Number forty-seven? Forty-seven."

Austin straightened. "That's me." He took several deep breaths.

"Break a leg." Leah smiled as she watched him head to the front. He spoke for a few moments with the table of people up front before settling himself upon the piano bench. His fingers immediately flew into a dazzling flurry. Leah marveled at his rendition of "Flight of the Bumble Bee." His body moved fluidly; his poise was exquisite.

"Wow." Tabitha sucked in a large bubble of gum. "He's pretty good."

Leah wondered what Tabitha's scale of excellence would be if she was ranking Austin at pretty good.

Austin came back over as number forty-eight was called.

"You were brilliant!" Leah clapped.

"Thanks," he said modestly.

The next person to audition was an older gentleman, who seemed technically flawless. "He lacks grace," Austin said with a click of his tongue. "Too bad because he plays beautifully."

"Number forty-nine?"

Leah's stomach clenched. Her knees felt like Jello as she stood. She had to remind herself to put one foot in front of the other. One step, two steps, and before she knew it, Leah was standing on the dais in front of the panel.

"Hello. Leah is it?" the large bald man asked. Leah could not get a good read on his attitude. She nodded hesitantly.

"My name is Clark McCauley. I am the director."

Recognition clicked. This was Tabitha's uncle, the director. Leah felt her anxiety kick up another notch.

"This is Paula, my choreographer, and Yasmine, one of my producers." He introduced everyone down the line. "Not that you care. We just want to see what you can do." He glanced at the clipboard again. "How long have you been playing, luv?"

"About twenty years?" Her voice croaked.

"And where have you played?" Clark's voice took a sudden condescending turn.

Leah froze, wondering if they were going to boot her out of the audition before she had a chance to play. "Church," she answered quietly.

They gave each other glances. She even caught a couple of eye rolls.

"Fine then." He heaved a bored sigh. "Go on. Have a seat. *Wow* us."

She sat stiffly at the piano, looking over the keys, imagining the tune in her head. Closing her eyes, Leah could almost hear Mrs. Jacobi chastising her about her posture. "Let the music set you free," she said quietly. "Let the music lift the weight of the world off your shoulders."

Scrapping the hymn she had planned to audition with, Leah began to play a lively Duke Ellington number. The song flowed through her, flooding her with memories of the last time she spoke with Jason...

It was the knock, his knock. Leah's heart began to race, but she was determined not to answer the door. She knew

*he stood on the other side with that damn smile and a bou-
quet of lilies to appease her.*

"I know you're in there, Leah." The loud knocking came
again. "You might as well open the door. I'm not going anywhere."

She wrestled with her conscience a few more seconds before she opened the door. "What do you want?"

"You won't return my phone calls so I thought an ambush
would be best." He thrust the bouquet forward with that
smile she had both loved and loathed.

"Keep them." She turned her back and walked further
into her apartment. "I can't do this anymore, Jason."

"Do what?"

"I am tired of the holding pattern you have me in. Waiting, hoping someday you might decide to settle down. Be
with me."

"I do want to be with you, someday."

"See! Right there! I can't do it anymore and now you
have a son and Rosa is in the picture. Everything is so incredibly complicated."

Jason stepped forward to embrace Leah. "I told Rosa I
am done, to pack her things and get out."

Leah could feel her body get tense. "I don't believe you."

With a nod, he dropped his arms. "She is at her parents'
house tonight. But I have to take steps to protect my son
before I can push the issue."

"And what about the others?" Leah stepped away from
him. "So you asked Rosa to move out. When are you going
to quit dating the other women?"

"I don't date other women when I am with you."

A scoff escaped her. "You were with Rosa when we were
together."

"I slept with Rosa when we were on one of our many
breaks." His voice raised a notch.

"We take so many breaks because you can't commit to
me." Her voice matched his.

"That doesn't mean I don't love you, Leah!"

They stood in shocked silence. She had waited so long to
hear those words from him, but now that they were out, they
didn't seem to make her as happy as she thought they
would.

"I love you," he said again. "I am not ready to commit,

but I want to make you happy." He offered the bouquet again.

Placing her hand firmly on his chest, she pushed him through the apartment. "You are not listening to me!" she said through clenched teeth. "I am done being your shadow. I am done waiting."

"But Leah," he pleaded.

She pushed him out the door. "Goodbye Jason." With a slam for good measure, Leah took a moment to catch her breath before she sunk to the floor in tears.

Waking the next morning, Leah splashed some water onto her swollen, puffy face. The evening before came back to her with startling clarity. Tears sprang to her eyes. Instead of giving in to the emotion, Leah threw on her running gear and headed out to clear her head.

The fresh morning air put her questions into perspective. She jogged along, enjoying the thump, thump of the pavement under her running shoes. Feeling the blood rush through her body, before she realized it, she had turned down Jason's street. Coming up to his house, she slowed to a jog and passed. Chastising herself for being stubborn, she turned around, made her way to the door, and knocked. Waiting a few moments, she knocked again. Jason answered fresh from the shower, wearing the fluffy blue robe she gave him for Christmas.

"Hey." He was unable to look her in the eye.

"I'm sorry," she said.

Stepping aside, Jason gestured for her to come in. "Want some coffee?"

"Water would be better." She followed him into the kitchen. The lilies looked as if they had been thrown into a vase. "You really should put these in water before they wilt and die."

He nodded. "I'll get to it." Handing over a glass of water, Jason poured himself a cup of coffee and headed out to the back patio. "You're right, you know," he said once they were settled. "About keeping you in a holding pattern, you're right. It is incredibly unfair of me to do this to you."

She felt the tears well up in her eyes. "Why?" She choked out the question. "Why did you wait so damn long to tell me you loved me?"

He shook his head slowly. "Love and hate are two very powerful words and I don't use them lightly."

Jason took a sip of coffee before he continued. His voice was sad, resigned, "I love you, Leah. I never meant to hurt you." He reached over, brushing his thumb across her cheek. "I love you, but want you to be happy." His thumb continued across her lips. "If moving on without me is what will make you happy, then so be it."

She leaned into his palm and closed her eyes, savoring his voice.

"You are the most amazingly talented, beautiful woman I had ever had the pleasure of knowing, Leah. You deserve to have someone hopelessly devoted to you. Someone who can give you everything you desire..."

Her audition had finished. The panel sat in stunned silence before Clark offered a thawed smile. "Thank you, luv," Clark said. "We will definitely be getting in touch with you."

Leah gave a small bow and felt for the first time as if she actually had a shot at this gig.

Austin stood and clapped as she approached. "Bravo! Beautiful form! What grace!"

She could feel the blush in her cheeks. "Well, thank you," she mumbled, her confidence soaring.

"Number fifty?" the voice announced. "Fifty."

Tabitha gave a bored sigh and headed to the stage. Leah's confidence plummeted again as she watched the freckled redhead seat herself at the piano. The fingers slammed down on the keys and made Leah cringe. Tabitha showed no heart for the music she played. The sound from the piano seemed choppy and forced. Clark McCauley seemed to make himself incredibly busy with the paperwork in front of him. When Tabitha finished, there was a polite murmuring and a hushed thank you. She came back to her seat to collect her magazines.

"I think you nailed it." Tabitha smiled at Austin and blew a bubble. "You were really good."

"Thanks," he said. "You were, err..." He turned to Leah for the right word before coming up with, "Definitely unique."

"Oh please!" Tabitha laughed, pushing her unruly hair into a ponytail. "I sounded like crap. The only reason I auditioned was to make my mother happy. She had been harping about this for weeks." Her voice took on a slightly bitter edge. "I was born into a musical dynasty, but the irony is I have no musical ability." She sighed, slinging a backpack over her shoulder, "The family keeps pushing and pushing, hoping by some miracle the music gene will kick in."

Although Leah was not overly fond of the woman standing in front of her, she could feel empathy for the familial push to be something she's not.

"So, Austin, do you want to go with me? To Red Rock Canyon?" she asked brightly. "It is absolutely *am-a-zing*! You will not regret it!"

He shifted uncomfortably, looking at Leah. "Um, I don't know."

"Go," Leah said with a laugh. "Have fun hiking! I am going to explore the city." She smiled. "Austin, I'll catch up with you later."

He looked like he wanted to protest, but Tabitha was pulling him to the door, chatting his ear off.

As Leah walked out of the ballroom, a weight began to lift off of her. She could do this, she decided. As she walked into the dry desert heat, the pulse of the city surrounded her. Whether she got the job or not, she conquered her first audition and felt a sense of accomplishment.

Jason had always believed in her and for the first time in her life, Leah began to believe in herself.

Chapter Twenty-Four

As Leah walked down Las Vegas Boulevard, she admired how one city could breathe so much excitement into the world. The tall buildings didn't seem as tall anymore and Leah felt as though she was on top of the world. She was finally making her dreams a reality.

Two men stood in front of the Venetian Resort talking about a poker tournament. It seemed gambling was a game that could be played anytime of the day. Life was not always about winning, but about taking chances. And Leah was taking a chance at living her dreams.

Catching sight of her reflection in the window of the café, Leah felt she would blend with the crowd of the Grand Lux Café at the Venetian Resort. Wearing her little black dress and a pair of red Jimmy Choo heels, an investment she was glad she made now, Leah entered the upscale restaurant with confidence.

"Welcome to the Grand Lux Café," a woman said with a coolly detached smile. "Will it be just you dining today?"

"No, I am meeting a friend for lunch, Mr. Austin Winter?"

Checking a hidden list, the woman nodded. "Of course, right this way."

The staccato of their heels clicked on the marble floor. Leah could hear people laughing, talking, and living in between the echo of her footfalls.

Austin stood when he saw her approaching. "Leah." His smile widened. "You look radiant." He caught her hand and lightly kissed her cheek.

"I am so glad I had a chance to meet with you before my flight leaves." Leah was pleasantly surprised to find a cup of coffee sitting in front of her. Sprinkling a yellow packet of sugar into the cup, she stirred lightly. The only reason she finally accepted his invitation for brunch was with a promise Tabitha would not be joining them.

"Have you heard anything yet?"

"No, not yet. I assume we won't hear anything for about a week or so." Austin sipped his coffee.

"I feel confident, but then again, a little uneasy. I don't think McCauley cared for me." She took a sip of coffee and savored the bitterness.

"Oh come on, lighten up. I think McCauley would choose you before he would even consider me," Austin said while looking over the menu.

"My flight leaves in a couple of hours and I am here, so you can save your charm. And just so we are clear, I do not put out on the first date." She smiled warmly, picking up the menu.

Austin blushed. "If I recall, I believe this is our second venture out. And although McCauley has a reputation for being a hard ass, he has an ear for natural talent."

The appearance of the waitress halted the conversation. Once they both settled on their order, their discussion resumed as if there had been no interruption.

"Leah, I don't think you realize how great of a pianist you are. You were amazing yesterday. I would have never guessed you were as nervous as you were. Imagine how phenomenal you will sound once you find your comfort zone."

Leah dismissed his compliment. "Well, I'm sure his niece would be his first choice. After all, Clark McCauley's sister really wants Tabitha to have the job."

Austin blushed at the mention of the redhead's name. "Tabitha has no interest in the gig. You heard her; she just showed up to appease her mother."

"Okay, but what about the other forty-six people who auditioned?" Leah could feel her confidence falter and changed the subject, determined not to ruin their meal with her negativity.

After they ate brunch Austin walked her outside. "Either way, there are always opportunities in the music industry. The important thing is to never give up on your talent," he said firmly.

"Thank you, Austin, for being such a fan. We have to stay

in touch." Leah smiled.

A limo pulled up alongside of them. The passengers began to unload and Leah recognized the judgmental faces of the audition panel. The last person to exit was Clark McCauley. He offered a polite nod to Austin before saying, "Lovely day, isn't it, Leah?"

The two watched the director disappear into the Grand Lux Café.

Austin leaned close and asked quietly, "Still think you didn't make an impression?"

Making his way to the front door, Calvin could hear the delighted squeals of his daughter from inside the townhouse. He was thankful that Marla was being so accommodating with his visitation.

"Daddy's here, Daddy's here!" The door rattled.

Marla's voice was quiet through the closed door, but still held a note of firmness. "What have I said about opening the door by yourself?"

"But Daddy's here!" The door flew open and Amanda plowed into her father with enthusiastic shrieks. "Daddy, Daddy, Daddy!"

"Well hello there, princess!" Calvin scooped up his daughter and held her close. She smelled of strawberries and crayons. "Are you behaving yourself?"

"But, but, it was you, Daddy!" She wrapped her arms around his neck and squeezed. "And I just missed you."

"Next time," Marla said sternly, locking the door behind them, "you wait for me."

"You need to listen to your mother." Calvin attempted the stern tone, but it fell flat and he gave his daughter a small wink. "Where is your brother?"

Cupping a hand over her mouth, Amanda leaned toward Calvin's ear and whispered loudly, "He is coloring a picture for Mommy's birthday tomorrow."

Marla shifted, looking around and pretending she didn't hear the secret. "Did you want to watch a little TV while Daddy goes to say hello to your brother?"

Amanda scrambled down and grabbed a DVD case.

"I would take that as a yes," Calvin laughed, heading down the hall to see his son. Knocking on the door, he opened it to find the quiet boy hunched over his desk. "Hey, champ, what are you working on?"

"Hi, Dad!" The boy's face lit up as he held up the drawing. "It's for Mom's birthday. What do you think?"

Calvin saw four figures juggling circles. "I think it is great. I had no idea you were such an artist."

"This is us eating ice cream because that is when Mom is the happiest. When we are eating ice cream."

Calvin nodded his head slowly. "Well don't let me interrupt you." He watched as his son pulled out a green crayon and methodically added the color to the head of the tallest figure. "I think you're right." He kissed the top of his son's head. "Maybe I should dye my hair green."

The strains of "Hakuna Matata" hit Calvin as he walked down the hallway. As much as he thought the song was irritating, he found himself humming along with the characters. When Calvin came into the living room, Marla was reading a book. Amanda was snuggled close sound asleep.

"Looks like someone is ready for bed," Calvin chuckled.

"Sorry," Marla said, pushing a button on the remote and silencing the movie. "I know you really wanted to spend time with the kids, but as you can see, one is working and the other..." She pointed to the quiet ball of energy.

"That's okay. I'll see them again tomorrow," he said, heading to the door.

"Wait? Did we have plans for tomorrow?"

Calvin locked eyes with his wife and gave her a slow smile. "I thought it would be nice for us to go get ice cream tomorrow. And since it is your birthday, you can have as many cherries as you'd like."

The adrenaline was still pumping through Leah's veins an hour after she left the plane. Climbing into her Mini Cooper, she dialed Calvin. The call went straight to voicemail. Two more attempts with the same result. She could feel the irritation tickle her until she realized she had no right to be irritated. Leah had blown Calvin off the last two days.

Digging out her cell again, she dialed Quincy. The gala loomed and Leah was sure that he would need a friend.

"Yeah?" he barked into the phone.

Leah was taken aback. It didn't sound like Quincy. Did he know that Leah knew about him and Claudia? No, that would be impossible. "Hey, Quincy, you okay?" she finally asked.

"Hey, Leah. I'm leaving the hospital, still no change in Tanvir's condition."

"Oh, that is awful!"

"His family is here so at least he has that, I guess." Leah heard a huge sigh. "But the gala is this weekend and it is a shame that he is going to miss everything we all worked for."

"It is the largest event ever for Bright Horizons and the university."

"I know." There was a moment of silence before Quincy continued. "Oh hey, would you mind helping out at the gala? Just a couple of hours. I really need some time to prepare my acceptance speech."

"Acceptance speech?"

"Yeah, Coach Turner is naming me his successor."

"Oh wow! Quincy, that is great news!" Leah laughed.

"Jason would be so proud of me. I always looked up to him. He was my role model. I wish he was here to see this," he said quietly.

Leah's breath caught at the mention of Jason's name. Not knowing what to say or how to respond, she sat waiting for Quincy to continue.

"I should get going. I have a meeting with Coach Turner," Quincy said quickly. "He will be upset if I'm late and I really don't want to incur his wrath."

"Really?" Leah said jokingly. "Coach Turner has a temper?"

"Oh, yeah, it isn't pretty," he answered seriously.

Leah's brain spun with the information. There was a long pause in the conversation.

"Leah?" Quincy said. "You still there?"

"Oh yeah, I'm here. Sorry, don't be late for your meeting. I will talk to you soon." Leah quickly hung up the phone. She drove home in silence, and wondered if Coach Turner really had a bad temper.

Chapter Twenty-Five

Coach Turner eyed the glass wall cabinet, shrewdly counting and reliving each award and trophy displayed behind the polished wood. Glancing at the clock, he couldn't help but shake his head in disgust. Quincy was late. How the hell was he expected to manage a top ten basketball team when he couldn't even make it to a meeting on time?

If it were up to Coach Turner, the job would have gone to someone else and Quincy would have been hired to clean the floors after the game. His brother-in-law insisted the job go to Quincy. He bent the university President's ear, and now Quincy had the job. Coach wondered if his brother-in-law knew about the affair.

He reminded himself to let it go for now. His pension depended on it. Until his retirement was official and the paperwork filed— he would put a smile on his face and play nice.

The knock on his office door interrupted his thought process. Quincy quickly entered and took a seat. "I am sorry, Coach. It has been really hectic around here lately with the gala coming up and all."

Coach thought Quincy was a complete waste of time, but the smile remained firmly on his face.

He even offered a nod of encouragement, but more than anything else, he wanted to snap Quincy's neck.

▌▌▌▌▌▌▌▌

Rosa picked up a dish towel to wipe the flour off her son's nose. He giggled, putting some on her cheek. She laughed with him, feeling lighter than she had in awhile. Rosa finished rolling out the dough and handed little Jay-Jay a teddy bear cookie cutter.

The sudden ringing of the doorbell caught her off guard. "Here, mijo." She tried to keep the nervous tension out of her voice. "You play with the dough. I'll be right back."

Before she could get to the door, it rang again. Looking through the peephole, Rosa rolled her eyes at the sight of Claudia. Holding her breath, she plastered a passable smile onto her face.

Claudia marched in as soon as Rosa opened the door. "Hello, Rosa," she said, air kissing Rosa's cheeks. "Don't mind me, I seem to have misplaced some documents that Jason signed." Claudia walked through the living room. "Something does smell delightful," she added over her shoulder.

Rosa almost sprinted to keep up. "Jay-Jay and I are making cookies. I wasn't expecting company."

"That is obvious," Claudia said, looking around. "I know you aren't working, dear." She wiped the flour off Rosa's face with her thumb and held her chin, turning the younger woman's face from side to side.

Rosa jerked her face out of Claudia's grasp.

"There really is no excuse to let yourself go," she said, continuing her way to the study.

Claudia gave a tsk at the door.

Rosa felt her anger rise. "What are you looking for?" she asked, keeping her temper in check. "Maybe I've seen it."

"Oh, Rosa, you are so darn cute!" Claudia rolled her eyes and began rummaging through folders on the desk. "You wouldn't know the first thing about what I am looking for." She knocked over a frame as she made her way to the bookcase. "Honestly, this room is a mess."

Rosa picked up the frame and looked at the smiling faces of Jason and her son. "Well between Jay-Jay running around and Leah breaking in..."

"Oh damn!" Claudia spun fast; a look of nervous anxiety crossed her face. "Did she take anything?"

Rosa shrugged, slowly enjoying Claudia's obvious discomfort. "I don't know. I haven't had a chance to go through here and take inventory."

Jay-Jay's voice called from the kitchen. "I'll be right there, mijo." Rosa turned back into the room. "I have a little boy needing me and cookies to bake so if you don't mind."

She gestured to the hallway.

Claudia smoothed down the front of her coat and followed Rosa into the living room. "Rosa," she said suddenly, "are you hiding something from me?"

"What would I possibly be hiding, Claudia?" she asked. "And even if I were, that would bring me to your level. I am nothing like you."

Her cheeks flushed through her layers of makeup. "He was only with you because he knocked you up. You know that, don't you?" Claudia smiled coldly.

Rosa could feel the heat of anger flame higher. "He only slept with you because you were an easy lay and a pay check."

Claudia opened her mouth, but Rosa held up her hand. "I don't want to fight with you, Claudia. We both know he only had room in his heart for one woman, Leah." She wrenched the door open. "Now please get out of my house. I have a son who needs me."

Claudia slid behind the wheel of her Mercedes, thankful for the tinted windows. She didn't want to give Rosa the pleasure of seeing her cry or seeing her makeup ruined by running mascara.

She had no idea why her emotions were getting the better of her; Claudia tried to get them under control as she sped down the street. Time was running out and she needed to get herself together.

Pulling out her cell phone, she scrolled through her address book until she found the number she wanted.

"Leah, darling. It's Mrs. Turner. How are you?" She turned at the corner. "Oh it has been one complication after another getting this gala underway." Claudia rolled her eyes listening to Leah. "I was wondering if you would be a dear and meet with me later this evening?" She paused, listening to the other end. "I know. I know you are busy, Leah, but I am asking you as a personal favor...for Jason." She waited a beat before adding, "This whole extravaganza is to honor his memory." Another beat before she added, "If it would be easier for you, I could come by your place. It won't take long. I want to go over the VIP list with you. Quincy said you would be willing to help." She resisted the urge to do a lady-like fist pump. "That would be fabulous, thank you, Leah. I will see you around eight-thirty." Claudia disconnected and threw her phone onto the passenger seat.

With a flick of her lighter, she lit a cigarette. Time was indeed running out and she needed that paper before the gala. She hoped that Leah had what she needed. Either way, a chat with Leah was way overdue.

Chapter Twenty-Six

Leah stared at the cell phone in her clammy hand.

"That didn't sound good," Calvin said, taking a bite of pasta. "Who was it?"

"Claudia," Leah choked out. Pocketing the cell, she took a deep, cleansing breath. "She wants to meet with me tonight."

Calvin slowly put his fork down. "Why?"

The sidewalk café where they were eating looked like a French postcard. It was reported to be the most romantic and chic place to entertain in the city, but Leah felt jittery despite the easy ambience. "She said she wanted to go over the VIP list for the gala."

He took another bite off his plate. "But you don't believe her?"

Picking at her salad, Leah felt there was more to the phone call. "Not really, no."

"I wish I could come over tonight, but I have this...birthday thing...to go to." His eyes remained fixed on his lunch.

Leah suspected there was more to the "birthday thing" than Calvin was letting on. But who was she to cast stones? She never told Calvin about the trip to Vegas. "It's okay," she said lightly. "Do your birthday thing. Claudia and I will have a nice cup of tea and discuss boring event planning stuff."

He seemed relieved. "Okay." Taking a look around, his smile brightened a little, but never quite reached his eyes. "This is a nice place."

Leah realized they only had a few dates left in their dwindling relationship. "It is," she responded politely as they sat in amiable silence, finishing their meal.

Nervously pacing around her apartment, Leah glanced at the clock and groaned. Claudia was due to ring her doorbell in ten minutes. She fluffed the pillows on her couch again and scanned the floor for a stray piece of lint—anything to keep her mind from spinning out of control.

Claudia said she wanted to talk about the gala. Leah wondered if that was really the case. She had bolstered herself up for an eventual confrontation on her terms, not Claudia's. Her stomach clenched in nervous anticipation as she shook the wrinkles from her curtains.

The sudden ringing of the telephone caused her to jump out of her skin. Leah contemplated not answering it, but then remembered that it might be Vegas. With a shaky hand, she answered with a very tentative hello.

"Leah?" Quincy's voiced rasped on the other end.

"Quincy? What's wrong?" She could hear the despair in his voice.

"Tan," he said. "Tan died this evening."

"What?" Her fingers flew to her crucifix and swung the gold emblem from side to side along the chain. "I thought he was stable? I thought..."

Quincy's sobs were heard through the line. "I don't know how to handle this, Leah. Two friends, two very close friends, gone. I don't know how to handle tragedy."

"What happened, Quincy?" She tried to keep the edge out of her voice.

"Doctors found high traces of potassium chloride in his blood panel. His heart stopped."

Leah's mouth went dry. First Jason, now Tanvir. Her body broke out in a cold sweat.

"The police also found the body of the night security guard in a dumpster behind the hospital. The guard was reported strangled to death." Quincy sobbed into the phone. "I don't know why all of this is happening."

The room started to spin and Leah closed her eyes as she tried to understand the tragic news, "Tanvir must of known something he wasn't supposed to," she said softly.

* * *

Numbers. Numbers were the key. Sitting behind the large oak desk, the man shuffled and worked with the numbers.

His favorite subject had always been math. It was consistent. It was a challenge, and one single number could change an entire equation.

The numbers needed to add up in his favor. Two people jeopardized the equation. He had no qualms about adding a third to his list.

Sitting back in the massive chair, his office door swung open slowly.

"I was wondering when you were going to show," the man said slowly, exhaling blue cigar smoke from his lungs. He offered a cigar to his visitor.

Declining the offer, the visitor headed over to the bar. "We had a few bumps along the road, but things seem to be progressing smoothly now," he said with a slight nod, pouring himself a double. "I do believe I will need a vacation, though, after the gala." He took a healthy swig. "Get away for a few days."

The man behind the desk snickered before inhaling on the cigar. "You can't take a vacation," he said calmly, the smoke curling around his head. "Our real work is just beginning." A supportive smile was given to his guest who paled visibly.

"What do you mean the real work?" The guest sank into a plush office chair. "I have been working my ass off for several weeks doing your bidding."

Blowing a stream of cigar smoke up to the ceiling, the larger man contemplated his choice of words, which must relate the severity of his position kindly.

"I have never had anything handed to me," he said calmly. "Hustled for everything I have. After the gala, I have some major numbers to work." He plastered a serene smile on his face. "I need the support of the university and Bright Horizons in order for me to press forward and do what I must do." He leaned forward. "The more the merrier."

The guest emptied his glass and headed to the bar for a refill. "I don't understand the nature of politics. You work and you work. What did Jason see in it?"

Rising up from behind the desk, the larger man walked slowly to the glass wall that looked over the city. "I have no doubt Jason would have won the election." He slid his hands into the pockets of his Armani pants. "He won the heart of the city. He was a stand up type of guy. Giving back to the community like he did, I respected him for that." A small tsk escaped him as he turned around. "Really is a shame he posed such a threat to my agenda. He could have done such great things."

Rolling his eyes, the guest drained his second glass. "This is why I don't get involved. I stick with basketball. It is a lot less messy."

The larger man's face twisted itself into a grimace. "You are involved, old friend. *You* committed the murders."

Chapter Twenty-Seven

The hard rap on the door caused Leah to jump and drop the phone she was holding. The conversation with Quincy so absorbed her she had almost forgotten Claudia was coming over. Leah picked up the phone from the floor, and noticed that Quincy was no longer on the other line. Before she could get to the door, the knock came again, more insistent than the original.

As Leah opened the door, she was hit with a wave of Channel No. 5. Claudia charged in, kissing the air in Leah's general direction. "Oh good, you are here." She smiled, which seemed forced. "I was beginning to wonder if you forgot our meeting." A gloved finger inched a small box closer. Claudia casually looked over the contents. "Going somewhere?"

It took a moment for Leah to find her voice. "I—my lease is up. I am moving."

"Mm-hmm." She glanced into another open box. "I see. Well, I can give you the name of a good cleaning lady." Claudia didn't look at Leah as she casually poked around a third box. "She might charge you extra, though." Rubbing her fingers together as if they were covered in dust, she continued. "Just a suggestion." There was the forced smile again as Claudia sat down on the couch. Bringing her large leather tote bag to her lap, she proceeded to pull out papers. "Let's get down to business, shall we?"

"Would you like some wine?" Leah asked, thinking that a drink might be what she needed to get through this meeting. Claudia was more intense than usual. It was obvious there was something else on her mind other than the VIP list.

"Red—dry red." Her perfectly lined lips parted as if to add

something else, but she began organizing the papers in her lap.

Leah headed to the kitchen to pour two large glasses of wine. Peering around the doorway to make sure Claudia couldn't see her, she took a couple of swallows out of the bottle. A little liquid encouragement, Leah reasoned, plugging the cork back into the bottle.

The wine glass was accepted and put aside as Claudia shuffled papers. "Now we have some politicians that you should recognize, a few school board presidents." She handed Leah a sheet of paper with profile pictures of the elite guests. "This man I would like you to keep an eye out for. Notify me immediately when he arrives."

Taking a large gulp of wine, Leah took the next sheet of paper offered to her and studied the well-dressed man in the photo.

"He is an old friend. I would like the opportunity to catch up with him before the madness of the gala sweeps us both up."

"Old friend, huh? Like Jason, old friend?" She hadn't realized she had spoken until she saw Claudia stiffen.

Not looking up from her papers, she answered a little too calmly, "He is a business associate, an attorney, if you must know."

Leah nodded, taking a small sip of wine. She had already irritated her guest; she decided to see how many buttons she could push. "I bet Coach is really looking forward to his retirement. He must be ecstatic. Not many people can retire at his age with such a large pension."

With a slightly shaky hand, Claudia reached for her wine. She took a sip and barely concealed a grimace.

"Oh my." She cleared her throat slightly. "That certainly is," Claudia cleared her throat again, setting the wine back on the table, "an interesting blend." She hunted through the sheaf of papers. "And as for your insinuation, my husband was fortunate enough to have a successful career with the university," Claudia said coolly. "He deserves to enjoy the fruits of his labor for the many years he has invested with the school." She looked up at Leah. "Speaking of husbands, how is the one you're sleeping with?"

Leah smiled through the hot blush in her cheeks. "My relationship with Calvin is just as casual as the one you have with Quincy."

"Touché, Leah." The perfectly painted face didn't crack. "I didn't come over here to bicker over trivial matters. I came to make sure the gala runs as smooth as possible." She handed over two more sheets of paper. "These two men need to be treated delicately."

"Would you like some more wine?" Leah asked abruptly, not taking the papers Claudia offered.

"No, thank you, dear. I still need to drive home." Claudia tossed the VIP list on the table next to the wine.

Leah went to the kitchen, refilled her glass of wine, and grabbed a slice of cheese out of the refrigerator. She could not judge how well this was going and had no clue why Claudia was here. Leah knew all of the people on the list at least by sight.

As she walked back into the living room, Claudia was emptying one of the larger packing boxes on the floor. "What are you doing?" She could hear her voice go up a notch with suspicion.

"I am looking for a document," Claudia said, thumbing through books. "The one you took from Jason's house."

"I have no idea what you are talking about." Leah shook her head in disbelief. Was this really happening? Her anger elevated swiftly. "Maybe you should be giving *me* some answers," she said. Her voice rose. "An explanation about the forged suicide note perhaps? Or maybe you know something about the death threat taped on my front door."

Claudia shook her head, a blonde lock falling into her face, giving her the look of irrationality. "I don't have time for this! I don't have time for your silly games." Her voice had an annoying shrillness to it. "I need to protect Jason's legacy before those money-grubbing hands get a hold of Bright Horizons and ruin *everything* we worked so hard for." She picked up another book and flipped quickly through the pages.

The hairline fractures in her perfect façade were apparent. Leah wasn't sure if she should be angry or feel sorry for the woman rooting through her things. "Come on, Claudia. I find it very hard to believe that you, of all people, give a crap about charity."

"Oh, this is absurd." Claudia dropped the book in her hand and picked up her bag from the floor. "Leah, there would have been a Bright Horizons even if I had never met Jason." Claudia tucked the stray lock of hair back into the French twist. "But he made it what it was. The community loved him, the media adored him." She pulled out her leather gloves and pulled them onto her delicate hands. "If I don't find that damn document, Jason and his legacy will be nothing but a very distant memory." Pushing her hair into place, she gave Leah a serious look before walking out of the apartment without looking back.

Leah stood in the middle of the disaster that once was her living room, wondering what document Claudia was looking for. Then she remembered the conch shell in Jason's office and the folder she had picked up before everything went black.

Putting the pieces together, Leah realized if Claudia was looking for the missing documents, the person who attacked her must have that folder.

Picking up the VIP list, Leah shuffled through the papers until she found the old business friend. Maybe she and Leo Grant, the attorney, should have a little chat before his arrival at the gala was announced to Claudia.

Calvin quickly checked his reflection in the glass next to the door. Smoothing down his hair, he was determined for his wife to take notice. Calvin was ready to come home to his family.

The steady *click, click* of heels on tile grew louder and Calvin's heart thumped loudly in his throat. He tried to keep his eagerness from showing.

"Hi," Marla said as she opened the door. Her smile was small, demure, and welcoming.

"You look great," he stammered, taking in the clinging red sweater and jeans.

She self-consciously ran her hands down her hips. "Thanks." She pointed to the bouquet of multicolored roses. "Beautiful flowers."

"Oh." He could feel the blush rise in his cheeks. "Sorry. These are for you." He handed them over with an awkward kiss to her cheek.

"Daddy!" Amanda shouted, racing to the door. "We can go get ice cream now?"

Calvin scooped her up into his arms. "Yes, princess, ice cream it is." He winked at Marla. "Maybe we should take Mommy bowling too."

"Bowling too!" Amanda screeched. "Tyler!" she yelled, tearing up the stairs. "Come on, Tyler, it's time to go!"

"Sorry for putting you on the spot like that," Calvin smiled as they waited for their bowling shoes. "It's your birthday and I wanted to do something fun."

Marla beamed, taking her size eight from the attendant. "I think I can forgive you." She sat next to her daughter, who struggled into the foreign shoes. "I might even wipe the lanes with you." Her eyes twinkled. It had been a long time since Calvin had seen a twinkle in his wife's eye.

"A wager?" Calvin laughed. "You think you can beat me?"

With a definite nod, Marla helped Amanda into her shoes. "I think I can annihilate you." She finished tying her daughter's laces and stood with confidence. "And when I do, you will buy me a whole jar of maraschino cherries."

"What do I get if I win?" Calvin asked, slipping the bowling shoes onto his feet.

"I'll give you a thimble," Marla said with a shy smile.

"Can we get the bumper pads?" Amanda took her mother's hand, oblivious to her parents flirting. "I want a pink swirl ball," she continued as they headed down toward their assigned lane.

With a thudding heart, Calvin realized that Marla offered him a kiss. He had forgotten how much they loved the story of *Peter Pan*. Apparently, she had not and was trying to tell him something. Or was she just being coy? He followed his son in the opposite direction. "What kind of ball are you looking for, champ?" Calvin asked, putting a gentle hand on his son's shoulder.

"I...am...looking...for..." he said, slowly running his hands over each ball they passed until he reached a neon green ball. Bright blue bowling pins were etched just above the small finger holes. "This one." He picked it up and rolled it around in his hands.

"Is it too heavy?" Calvin asked, watching his son slide his fingers into the holes and swing the ball slightly back and forth.

"Nope, it's perfect." Tyler smiled.

Marla's laugh permeated through the alley. They looked to see Amanda trying to throw a ball between her legs. "Well, your mother and sister seem to be having a good time."

"If Mom is this happy now," Tyler said with a shake of his head, "she is going to be bouncing off the walls when we have ice cream!"

The silence in the car on the way home was amicable and nerve-wracking. The kids had fallen asleep. It was the perfect time to talk with Marla about his feelings, but Calvin could not get over his nervousness.

She sat close enough to touch. All he had to do was reach his hand out and hold hers. The jar of cherries Marla held almost covered her lap, but he could still get to her hand.

"Did you have a good birthday?" he asked quietly.

Marla laid back against the headrest, keeping her eyes out the side window. "It was the best birthday ever."

"Dad?" Tyler roused himself from his nap. "Can we do this again, but before Mom's next birthday?"

"We sure can, champ," Calvin chuckled. "I need to try and win my thimble."

Lapsing back into the silence, the war continued in Calvin's head. As he pulled into the driveway, Calvin had talked himself out of telling Marla anything tonight. They had a fun family evening with a lot of laughter and banter. Why ruin it?

He unbuckled Amanda, carried her into the house, and tucked her into bed. Calvin popped into Tyler's room and kissed him goodnight. Making his way downstairs, he found Marla in the kitchen. "Kids are out," he chuckled nervously. "I, uh, happy birthday and goodnight."

"Wait," Marla called out. "I...do you want some tea?"

"It's late," Calvin replied, trying not to look into his wife's eyes. He wanted her more than anything and looking at her made his heart ache.

"Please, stay." She poured out two mugs and pushed one across the counter.

Calvin slid onto a bar stool and slowly spun the mug in between his hands. "So when you said this was the best birthday ever..."

"I lied." Marla sighed with a smile. "This was the second best. The best birthday ever was ten years ago. The night you proposed."

With misty eyes, his brain went into overdrive. There was so much he wanted to say, but didn't know where to start.

Marla slid her hand across the counter, covering his large one with her soft, smooth one. "Please stay tonight. I love it when you're home." Calvin now flooded with emotion, was confused. Did his wife have a change of heart? He sat there for a moment in silence looking at the woman he had once promised to love for the rest of his life. Calvin smiled; he was glad to be home.

Chapter Twenty-Eight

Applying a bit more lipstick, Leah considered her appearance in the full-length mirror. Her head still reeled from the confrontation with Claudia.

The last thing she wanted to do was give Quincy clothing advice.

His nervousness was understandable. This was a huge deal for him and he wanted to look presentable. She advised him to wear a standard bow tie with his tux and quickly hung up the phone.

Grabbing her keys and clutch, Leah checked herself in the mirror one more time. She chewed on her bottom lip, wondering if coral was too bold a choice. Maybe she should stick to the traditional black, blend in a little better. Her stomach lurched. The last thing she wanted to do was stick out tonight. The clock decided for her. She was running late and settled on the long coral dress.

On her way over to the convention hall, Leah went over the guest list in her head and recalled the photo of the attorney she was to look out for. As she pulled her Mini Cooper up to valet parking, the nerves in her stomach had turned to nausea.

People milled on the marble steps leading up to the building. Designers from all over the world were represented by the looks of the dresses worn in honor of Jason. It looked as if a fashion runway was underway instead of a gala.

Leah quickly made her way to the VIP table. She said hello to a few people she passed and was relieved to see extra security around the hall. There still was a crazed killer out there.

Detective Becky nodded a greeting from a side door as Leah situated herself at the table. Rosa brooded in a corner, glaring at anyone who dare approach her. Leah did have to admit Rosa looked pretty in a dusty mauve off-the-shoulder dress. If only she smiled a little.

Halfway across the room, the governor laughed with the university president and several other people whom she didn't recognize, but still seemed important enough to belong in the political circle. The mayor held court a few feet over as he slapped the shoulder of a noteworthy politician. Leah could not for the life of her remember the gentleman's position.

"Excuse me?" A low voice broke into her thought process.

Leah's head swiveled and settled on the attorney, Leo Grant. "Mr. Grant!" she said loudly, offering her hand.

He took it reluctantly. "Have we met?"

Feeling the slow burn of embarrassment, Leah shook her head. "No, sir." She looked around the hall and did not see Claudia. She searched for Quincy. Maybe he might know where Claudia was. But Quincy was also missing. That didn't sit well with her. It didn't seem right that they were both absent.

"No sir, we have not met." Leah looked around again. "But I have been instructed to deliver you to Mrs. Turner when I found you." Leah linked her arm through Leo Grant's. "Let's take a stroll and see if we can find her." She offered her most sincere smile.

Claudia parallel parked her car and knew in her heart that the papers were here. After tonight, she would no longer be the coach's wife. All her life she'd spent fading in her brother's shadow. Now it would be her turn to shine. She and Jason had built Bright Horizons and no one would take it away. Not even her selfish brother who had only invested to boost his political image. Claudia could feel the bile inch into her throat.

Casually walking up to the front door, she shook out her keys and slid one into the lock. Her heart beat faster at the click of the tumblers, letting her know the door was unlocked.

Sighing with relief, Claudia slipped into the front room

and closed the door, thankful she had the foresight to steal the spare key from the garden and make a copy. The house seemed too familiar and a little too quiet.

With the gala underway, she didn't have much time to spare. Making her way down the hall, she passed the bed-room, not glancing at the bed she had spent so many hours in with the enemy. Sacrificing her dignity and pride, Claudia used her body to keep tabs on the one person who could de-stroy her.

Confidently walking into the office, Claudia had the un-easy sense that she wasn't alone. She quickly glanced around and decided she was just being paranoid. Feeling her way behind a large oak bookcase, her fingers closed around the small safe key.

The document had to be here, she thought, holding the key to her chest. As she turned, a small noise in the hallway stopped her. Cold sweat beaded across her forehead. Listen-ing, she heard nothing out of the ordinary and continued on to the large safe in the corner.

Sliding the key into the lock, she turned it, and for the second time that evening, Claudia felt relief that all was go-ing according to plan. Quickly leafing through the folders and documents, Claudia pulled out a manila envelope. Unclasping the back binder, she thumbed through the papers inside. Her heart leapt with joy. This was it! She had found the docu-ments.

Folding the envelope, she shoved it into her clutch. Clau-dia looked up at the doorway and gasped in fear.

It was the enemy she had spent so many hours in bed with. He stood in the doorway with an evil grin and a gun, dressed in a tuxedo with a traditional bow tie.

Chapter Twenty-Nine

"We have an awe-inspiring year ahead of us," the president of the university announced after he took the stage. A polite spattering of applause filled the room. Leah obliged by clapping slowly, her eyes roaming the room. She sensed something was not right.

"Our past success is due in large part to our wonderful mayor. Without him, we would not be where we are today." The applause began again.

Leah did not join in as she realized Claudia and Quincy still had not arrived.

"The mayor is an educational leader," the president continued. "Bright Horizons has a real future with him in office."

A door opening distracted Leah. She turned to watch the mayor pat Leo Grant on the shoulder. They exited the hall together, laughing. Leah could not contain her anxiety as she moved through the room, looking for Detective Becky.

"Hi, Leah," she said quietly. "Are you all right?"

Leah shook her head no. "Something doesn't feel right. Quincy and Mrs. Turner never arrived."

Becky stood straighter. "I'll send a squad over to the Bright Horizons Youth Group headquarters to check it out, okay?"

With a nod, Leah wandered back into the crowd. Try as she might, she could not concentrate on what the president of the university was saying. Earlier, Mrs. Jacobi had whispered in her ear, "People aren't always what they seem."

Claudia and Quincy did make a very odd couple. Maybe the Bright Horizons office wasn't the place to look. Surprised by her sudden determination, Leah exited the hall and went out into the still night air.

"I don't understand, Quincy." Claudia could feel the sting of tears and for once, did not care that crying would ruin her makeup. "Why you? Why this?" Her wrists chafed against the rope as she struggled to get a hand loose.

"It won't work." He sat heavily into a leather wing back chair. "My knot tying skills are legendary." His chuckle sent a shiver down her spine. "You aren't going anywhere."

"Why are you doing this to me?" Her shoulders ached from the unnatural position of having her hands tied behind her back.

"Because, my dear Claudia, you need to realize that you are not in control." He brought the gun up. It glistened in the light from the fireplace. "Before I kill you, that is."

Tears ran down her cheeks freely. She was going to die. "Quincy, *please*! Talk to me. What can I do to help?" Claudia wasn't going down without a fight.

"Nothing." He stood slowly. His eyes glinted like the steel of his gun. "You have done enough."

Taking a step closer, Claudia shrank against the chair. He caressed the gun against her cheek. "This would have been easier if you had left it alone."

"I...I..." she stammered, and hated the fear she felt. "Left what alone?"

"Bright Horizons. It is mine. Your brother made sure of it."

"My...brother?" Claudia could not believe what he was saying. "What does he have to do with this?"

Quincy chuckled again and poured himself a drink. "He hired me to kill Jason. Put me in the position to take over for your husband and Bright Horizons." He stared into the fire. "I was going to kill Jason in his office. Make it look like a suicide. Even had the note planted, but it didn't work out so I had to think of a plan B."

"The suicide note Rosa found?"

"Yeah, I forgot to get it back. She is a smart cookie, figured out what we were up to."

Claudia exhaled slowly, wondering why she didn't see it sooner. "She blackmailed you."

"And the mayor," Quincy nodded. "How else do you think she could afford not to work and continue to live in that neighborhood? It sure wasn't Jason's generous will." He chuckled, turning back to Claudia. "Jason told me that if anything ever happened to him, the kid was to live with his parents, not with Rosa."

"At least you could have done that for him." Claudia began working at the knots with a bit more discretion.

"That would have meant bringing forth the will and then where would I be?" An evil smile played about Quincy's lips. "I was instructed to burn the will, but I couldn't bring myself to do it. What if your brother turned on me? That will is my insurance policy."

"So your plan B?" Claudia asked. If only she could shift her body in the straight-backed chair she might gain enough leverage to get a hand free.

"Plan B," he said proudly. "Plan B started to unravel before it began. Leah showed up at his house just as I did and I had to wait for her to leave. Then he put up a fight." Sitting back down in the chair, he took a sip of scotch before he continued. "In the struggle, I dropped the gun and I had to stab him. The scene was a little gruesome. You were the one who put a bright spot on my plight." His grin made her skin crawl. "You called as he took his last breath and I had the idea to stage it as a lovers' quarrel."

Claudia's stomach churned with revulsion. She could not imagine how anyone could be so callous to talk about murder in such a way.

"How did my brother get involved?"

"Politics, Claudia," Quincy said with a slow shrug. "Jason wanted to run for mayor. Your brother knew that Jason would win without even trying, so I was brought in to smooth the waters, so to speak."

"But he was your best friend."

His laughter rang through the room. "Not really, no. Jason never had to work for anything. It all came so easy to him. Me? I had to struggle, fight for everything I have. Your brother gave me an opportunity to quit fighting and I took it."

The sound of a car door out front ceased the conversation. Quincy was on his feet in an instant, hurrying to the front window. With the gun firmly in his hand, he pushed open the heavy drape to look outside. "Oh, how incredibly sweet." His voice dripped with contempt. "Your savior has arrived."

Heavy rapping on the front door stopped Claudia's breathing. Quincy puts his finger to his mouth as he tiptoed over. Standing against the door, he extended his arm, waiting for the unexpected visitor to enter without invitation.

The door opened slowly. "Claudia?" Coach Turner stepped across the threshold.

"No! Barry! Wait!" Claudia cried, getting her hands free.

Coach turned to see Quincy pointing the gun at him.

Claudia raced across the room.

A shot rang out.

Leah turned down Quincy's street, not sure of what she was going to find. Claudia and Quincy both not showing up to the gala did not bode well. Quincy was being announced as the new head coach for the university. How could he not show up?

And Claudia always needed a reason to shine. The past galas had been the pedestal she would place herself on. This one was the biggest and most important. Something had to be wrong.

Pulling up to Quincy's house, she saw the sleek black Mercedes out front. How did she miss Coach Turner not being at the gala? And what was he doing here? She quickly parked. The sound of gunshots made her curl up into a ball. Her heart thudded so loud it almost drowned out the next two shots that came from Quincy's house. She waited a bit until all was quiet. Pulling out her cell phone, she dialed 911 to report shots fired and to request Detective Becky.

She stayed crouched for several minutes more, debating whether to wait outside or investigate the gunshots. Curiosity won out and Leah walked over to the house.

The windows were covered; she could not hear a noise when she pressed an ear up to the glass. Leah tiptoed around to the front door and found it slightly ajar. Pushing it open slowly, she stepped over the threshold and listened again. Crying came from the living room. Leah crept quietly down the hallway.

"Seriously, Leah?"

She froze mid-step. Turning around, she saw Quincy standing behind her, the gun firmly by his side.

"What the hell are you doing here?"

"Quincy?" she asked uncertainly. "What is going on?"

He shook his head. "All this time I tried to keep you safe, keep you out of this."

Shaking her head, she took a small step back. "What are you talking about?"

"Jason left Bright Horizons to me," Claudia said from the doorway. There was a panicked tone to her voice that made Leah more fearful.

Leah's hand went to her mouth to silence the scream bubbling to the surface. Claudia's cream-colored Marchesa gown was splattered in blood.

"I don't understand." Leah could feel the tears behind her eyes.

"The manila envelope you found in Jason's office." Quincy sighed. "It held the original will. That is why I knocked you on the head. I never wanted you involved. I wanted you to go to Vegas and forget all of this. I left that note on your door to get you out of here."

"You left the death threat?"

"He killed Jason too," Claudia said. There was a note of defeat in her voice.

Leah felt her eyes grow wide. "You killed Jason?" The room started to spin. Leah had to fight to stay standing, to find out the truth. "Did you kill Tanvir too?" She looked at Claudia. "Are you okay?" she asked slowly, pointing at the red spray across her dress.

"I need to get an ambulance for my husband," Claudia said, cutting Quincy with a look. "Did you kill Tanvir?"

Quincy nodded. "I had no choice. I tried to attack him in his office, but he struggled and there were cleaning ladies roaming. I had to wait for the perfect opportunity to go back to the hospital and inject Tanvir with potassium, creating an instant heart attack." An arrogant grin came across his lips. "Unfortunately I had to take care of the security guard who I bribed to let me in."

"Why?" Leah asked hesitantly.

"Tanvir was one of the witnesses to the original will and he wanted my job as head coach."

Leah felt overwhelmed with too much information. Her knees turned to jelly and she found it difficult to stay upright. "What's wrong with Coach Turner?" She asked after regaining control.

"Quincy clipped his leg," Claudia said as a tear ran down her cheek. "Shot him without warning."

From her vantage point, Leah could see the flashing lights of the squad cars pull up. She breathed a sigh of relief that there was no siren fanfare announcing their approach.

The police station was cold and damp. Leah's body shivered in the hard plastic chair she sat. Her brain swam with the information that she had been given.

Steady footfalls broke into her concentration as relief flooded through her. "Thanks for coming," Leah said, standing slowly. "I wasn't sure who to call."

Calvin put his arm around her waist for support. "What happened?"

She put a shaky hand to her head. "Oh my gosh, Quincy killed Tanvir and Jason, the mayor's been arrested, Leo Grant, and Quincy too. And Coach Turner's been shot." Leah looked up at Calvin. "It has been a very long night."

"Sounds like it." Calvin opened the passenger side door for Leah and helped her in. "How are you holding up?"

"Nothing a very long hot shower and a bottle of Pinot Noir won't fix." She smiled sadly. "I am so sorry I called."

"Please don't apologize. I am here because I want to be." He shut the door and ran around to the driver's side. "Where would you like me to take you?"

"My car is still at Quincy's, but I'm not sure if I am ready to go back there, so if you could just take me home, that would be great." She laid her head against the seat. "It's funny; I thought I would feel better knowing the truth about Jason's murder."

"You don't?" Calvin asked, pulling onto the street.

She shook her head. "I feel surprisingly empty." She sighed, closing her eyes.

Chapter Thirty

Leah entered the church for Tanvir's funeral. Another friend gone, but at least the secret had been unraveled. Jason, as well as Tanvir, could now rest in peace. She shook her head at the two innocent lives lost because of jealousy and greed.

Claudia waved to her and came over. Dressed in a conservative black dress and simple heels, Leah felt a little dowdy next to the older woman's fashion forward sense of style and excess.

"Oh, Leah." Claudia held out her hands as usual, but instead of the air kisses they usually exchanged, she engulfed her in a Chanel-infused embrace. "It is so good to see you!"

With a little cough, Leah released her new friend and took a step back. "It is good to see you too," she said. "How have you been?"

Claudia waved her hand dramatically. "Busy, busy, I have such wonderful plans for the future of Bright Horizons. Everything Jason dreamed and more." A flicker of sadness crossed her face before she resumed her upbeat tone. "Some ideas were his anyway, most are mine, but all the same, Bright Horizons has a very bright future."

Coach Turner limped into the sanctuary. He smiled at the ladies before taking a seat close to the front.

"How is he doing?" Leah dropped her voice a notch.

Claudia's eyes followed her husband until he was safely situated. With a sigh, she answered, "Well, he has come out of his very short retirement until the university can find a suitable replacement for him. There is probably another year of coaching ahead of him. Other than that..." She shrugged casually. "His leg is healing fine."

They silently watched others file into the church: business colleagues, school friends, family.

"Oh, did you hear?" Claudia said, taking a step closer.

"What?" Leah asked, startled out of her silent reverie.

"Rosa was arrested." Her eyes twinkled with evil mischief.

Leah's eyes blinked rapidly. "Arrested? For what? Where's little Jay-Jay?"

"Blackmail and failing to report a murder." She looked around before continuing. "Little Jay-Jay is fine and living with Jason's parents."

"Which is what Jason wanted to begin with." Leah said with relief.

After the service, Leah wandered down to the park across the street. The weather was beautiful: sunny, and mild. She inhaled the sweet air and was thankful for the splendor of nature. Leah spotted two kids playing ball across the park, laughing and enjoying each other's company. The parents were sitting on a park bench close by wrapped up in each other.

She thought it was nice to see two people so attentive to each other, and it made her think that there was hope for her. Maybe she could... The woman shifted to look at the kids. Leah felt as if the wind had been knocked out of her as she saw Calvin's face clearly next to the woman.

Why hadn't he said anything? She wondered. Her feet wanted to run, run away from the man who'd played with her heart and emotions. The man who'd made her believe that there might be a happily ever after.

A ball came rolling to her feet. Leah looked into the face of Calvin's little girl. Amanda, was it? She had his smile. Looking up, Leah's eyes locked with Calvin's. She inclined her head in acknowledgement. Without saying a word, it was clear that this was goodbye.

Calvin stood in his bedroom and shrugged himself into his sport coat. Splashing some aftershave onto his face, he eyed himself in the full-length mirror from every angle.

Marla was in the kitchen loading the dishwasher. "Good

luck on your poker game tonight." she smiled as her husband came downstairs to grab his keys. "What time will you be home?"

Pulling her into a strong embrace, he kissed her. "I'll only play a couple hands," he said. "Who knows? I might win big tonight. Maybe enough to go on a little mini vacation?" He wagged his eyebrows at her. "Just the two of us?"

"Sounds heavenly," Marla laughed trying to hide the tightness in her voice.

Climbing into his SUV, Calvin pulled out his cell and began to scroll through numbers. He paused at Leah's name. The look she gave him this afternoon left no question in his mind. It was definitely over between them.

With a sigh, he deleted her number and scrolled down until he found the one he was searching for. The woman he met at the café the weekend that Leah blew him off during her business venture.

"Hey," he said into the phone. "I'm leaving now. I'll see you soon." His face broke into a small smile. "I know. I can't wait either."

Marla watched through the window as the lights from Calvin's vehicle faded down the street. Her heart was already broken. It had broken the first time Calvin cheated on her and never fully repaired itself. She knew he would never change. For once, she was ready to accept reality.

Grabbing her pills, Marla checked in on her children. Both fast asleep. She could not resist kissing them and tucking the blankets around them again before she drew her bath.

Walking into the restroom, the reflection in the mirror caused her to stop. To her surprise, Marla saw a woman of strength, a woman who was not scared to love herself. Opening the bottle of pills in her hand, she flushed the remaining Xanax tablets down the toilet and tossed away the empty bottle.

As she climbed into the scorching tub, Marla thought of Calvin and felt too numb to even notice the heat against her flesh. He was right about one thing; a mini vacation would be nice. That is why Marla had purchased three tickets for her and the kids to get away for a few days. The thought of palm trees and seashells reminded Marla that she had to finish packing their suitcases. Their flight would leave at sunrise. She already knew her husband had no plans of coming back home tonight, but in the morning he would come home to an empty house with divorce papers waiting on the kitchen counter. Marla had talked to her attorney, one of the best in the state, and he promised to have a court date scheduled when she returned.

She closed her eyes and guided her soapy hands across her face and down the base of her neck. She could feel the pulse beating through her skin. She was still alive, and that meant she still had a chance to start a new life. Marla smiled, and all the pain seemed to wash away.

Leah sat at the piano, plinking out notes. She was sounding out a tune she had heard the other day when the phone rang. She chose to ignore it. There was no one she wanted to talk to. It was probably her mother and she definitely did not want to talk to her mother.

The answering machine clicked on. Leah recognized Clark McCauley's voice immediately and dove for the phone.

"Hello? Hello?" She could hear the screech in her voice and took a small breath.

"Allo, luv, did I catch you at a bad time?"

"No, sir, no. I'm good." She felt a nervous giggle come on. "What can I do for you?"

"Aye, luv, well, rehearsal starts this weekend. You need to learn the score before we open in two weeks."

"I got it?" She bit her tongue hard. She needed to sound a bit more professional. "I mean, yes, I can fly in Friday."

"Excellent, luv, see you then." Leah hung up the phone and gave in to the exuberance. "I got it, I got it, I got it!" she screamed, jumping around the piles of boxes.

She collapsed on the piano bench, still feeling as if she were on cloud nine as she slid Mrs. Jacobi's letter off the top of the piano. Leah could finally feel her dreams at her fingertips.

Leah was surprised her hands weren't shaking as she applied the last of her makeup. Opening night butterflies were running rampant in her stomach. The light knock on the door made the butterflies leap.

"Oh my!" she exclaimed taking the flowers hovering before her face. "What are you doing here?"

Austin beamed and offered her a light hug. "Did you think for one moment I would miss your debut?" He took a step back. "Don't let me deter you. Finish getting ready," he said, looking over his shoulder. "Tabitha was nice enough to sneak me back here." His voice lowered a notch. "But I better hurry back to my seat so I can watch you play."

Leah blushed almost the same color as the roses she held.

"Would you mind?" He cleared his throat. "Joining me for a late dinner after the show?" His eyes looked a bit hopeful. "I would love to catch up with you."

"Why Mr. Winter," she said in mock surprise, "are you asking me out on another date?"

He nodded solemnly, "I do believe so, ma'am."

"I think that would be lovely."

He kissed the top of her head and told her to break a leg before he hustled down the hallway.

On the big stage, Leah sat behind the grand piano glancing at the crowd of elegantly dressed. Tonight was her first performance in Vegas and she had mastered every song one after the other. The hot stage lights seared her skin, but suddenly, there was a chill in the air.

She closed her eyes before her fingers hit the first key.

This was the last song to a perfect performance. When she opened up her eyes, the ghosts from her past sat among the crowd. Quincy, Tanvir, Coach Turner, Claudia, Rosa, Marla, and Calvin were there in spirit, reminding Leah what she had walked away from. A wave of nausea hit. Her eyes caught Mrs. Jacobi standing off stage, tapping out the beat with her hands as she often did softly, fingertips to palms. She looked like a proud teacher in the wings. The nausea began to subside.

Leah felt her hands tremble as she saw Jason sitting in the audience, but she managed to continue her performance without faltering.

Her fingers flawlessly flew across the eighty-eight keys of ivory. A look of pride etched across Jason's handsome face. She shut her eyes tight, so tight her lids ached. When she opened them again, he was gone.

His tall, muscular form was spotted again halfway up the aisle. Jason turned and gave her a smile. It was the same smile that made her heart melt and her blood boil. He mouthed, "I love you" before turning and walking out of the theater.

She turned back to the keys in time to watch her fingers pound out the final notes of the finale. A thunderous applause erupted throughout the theater. The faces of her past faded one by one from her view. Her present remained. Her mother and father often went unnoticed in Leah's world, but that night, they were on their feet, front and center, applauding their daughter. She saw Austin who looked up at her in amazement as he let out a loud whistle of praise.

The burgundy curtain began to close, creating a thick velvet wall between her past and her future.

Leah smiled.

Her life was now beginning.

About the Author

Catherine Lavender is a writer and poet. She is a member of the Florida Writers Association, as well as an animal activist in her local area. She is a devoted supporter of the organization First Book which helps supply literature for underprivileged children. In her spare time, Catherine enjoys reading classic literature and playing the acoustic guitar. She is from Baltimore, Maryland but now resides in Tampa, Florida with her beloved dog.